Douglas Wynn spent [...] and Bedfordshire. A[...] degree in Chemistry [...] for many years as a rese[...] technical college lecturer. He retired early to concentrate on his writing and his interest in criminology. An adult-education tutor in creative writing and a member of the Society of Authors, he has written many articles on true murder cases and a wide collection of books on the subject. In 1988, he wrote *Settings for Slaughter*, in which the locations of various crimes were shown to have a marked effect on the outcome of the cases. The author lives in Lincolnshire.

Also by Douglas Wynn in Futura

SETTINGS FOR SLAUGHTER: THIRTEEN MACABRE MURDERS

BLIND JUSTICE?

Ten Killers Who Almost Got Away
With Murder

Douglas Wynn

Futura

A Futura Book

First published in Great Britain in 1990
by Robert Hale Limited

This edition published by
Futura Publications in 1992
a Division of
Macdonald & Co (Publishers) Ltd
London & Sydney

ISBN 0 7088 4965 2

Printed and bound in Great Britain by
BPCC Hazell Books
Aylesbury, Bucks, England
Member of BPCC Ltd

Futura Publications
A Division of
Macdonald & Co (Publishers) Ltd
165 Great Dover Street
London SE1 4YA

A member of Maxwell Macmillan Publishing Corporation

Contents

Acknowledgements

I extend my grateful thanks for their help to the staff of the Hereford and Worcester County Records office; to Paddy Burgess, curator of the Museum of Lincolnshire Life; to Bryan Berryman and staff at the North Yorkshire County Library; and to Mrs Mavis Davies at the Local Studies Library in Guildford.

For permission to quote from *Murder in France* by Alister Kershaw I am happy to thank the publishers, Constable, and for permission to quote from the *Southport Guardian* of 28 June 1947 I am grateful to the group editor, Southport Visitor Series, Newspapers Ltd.

I would also like to thank *The Times* for permission to use reports in that newspaper on 29 January and 14 February 1963. Extracts from the *Evening News*, Portsmouth, and the *Hampshire Telegraph* and *Post* appear by courtesy of *The News*, Portsmouth.

The confessions of Donald Hume originally appeared in the *Sunday Pictorial* and I am grateful to the editorial manager of the *Sunday Mirror* for permission to use this material. And I am also indebted to Mirror Group Newspapers for permission to make use of material appearing in the *People* in December 1960 and May 1963.

Introduction

Bernard Taylor and Stephen Knight in their book *Perfect Murder* (1987) make the point that the really ideal murder is one which is simply not recognized as such. There is no police investigation and the murderer is safe in the knowledge that nobody is looking for him. The death is viewed as being due to natural causes, or suicide, or perhaps it is not even known about – the victim has simply disappeared and no one, except the murderer, knows what has happened to them. But because of their very nature we know nothing about these cases.

Another category of perfect murder is the unsolved crime: Murder has manifestly been committed, but no one is actually brought to justice. Very often no one is even brought to trial and the murder remains a complete mystery. Although many of these cases are quite interesting I find them less than satisfactory. I like to know, or at least have a very strong suspicion, who perpetrated the crime.

In this book, therefore, I have only included cases where we know who was responsible, even though the murderers were able, at least initially, to avoid the consequences of their crimes. In some instances they were found not guilty at the trial, but afterwards confessed. Sometimes, for various reasons, they were never tried for the crime at all, although the evidence against them was overwhelming. And in one instance the murder charge was reduced to manslaughter.

But in all the cases I have chosen, although the perpetrators got away with murder, justice, in one form or another, caught up with them in the end.

In one instance the murderer was found not guilty at the trial, but years later unwisely sued for libel the author and publishers of a book which seemed to question the verdict, and lost his case. He afterwards confessed to the crime. Some others, after being found not guilty, went on to commit other murders for which they were convicted. Another committed suicide before he could be brought to trial, but the jury at the inquest on his victim convicted him, in his absence, of murder. Two others having been found not guilty finished up in lunatic asylums; and one, an early hit-man, was subsequently disposed of by his employers.

In some stories I have been able to offer an alternative explanation of the facts to the usually accepted one. In the Setty murder, for example, Hume's confession is in many places at variance with the facts, and although he almost certainly did murder Setty, he probably did not do so in the way he describes.

Similarly, all the accounts I have read of the murder of Eric Tombe ignore the fact that there were two women in his life, not one. And the reconstruction I suggest helps to explain why one of them, who went so far as to threaten the murderer, Ernest Dyer, with going to Scotland Yard, did not apparently do so.

All this allowing us to echo John Dryden's words: 'Justice is blind, he knows nobody.'

1 Donald Hume:
A Drop in the Ocean

Donald Hume was going to commit the perfect murder.

But, as he climbed the narrow stairs to his second-floor flat, he looked over his shoulder at the short, heavily built man following and for a moment a doubt assailed him. The man was much bulkier than him. Would he be able to overpower him?

Then the voice of the big man, Stanley Setty, broke into his thoughts, its accent betraying the man's Middle Eastern origins. 'I can't spare you much time. I want to look at a Jag in Watford tonight.'

They continued their way up the stairs.

It was 4 October 1949, and London had a black market flourishing in practically everything. Stanley Setty operated in this sphere. Ostensibly he was a second-hand car-dealer with his business centred on Warren Street and Great Portland Street. And like many other traders in the area he conducted his business in the local cafés and pubs.

But Setty dabbled in anything that was in short supply. He was also well known as a kerbside banker, cashing cheques – for a substantial fee – for people who didn't have a bank account, and this entailed his carrying large sums in cash. In fact on this particular day, a Tuesday, he was known to have over a £1,000 in five-pound notes in his pocket.

Setty often supplied customers with particular makes and years of cars by simply having agents steal the vehicles, and Donald Hume had supplied him with several stolen cars in the past few months. Hume was a similar operator in the black market, but he was markedly less successful than the bulky man from the Middle East and resented his prosperity.

They eventually reached the landing where Hume had his flat and he opened his front door. Inside was a very small hall, and off to the right, a door led into a lounge. A large room, it had three windows on the longest wall which overlooked the Finchley Road, quite near to Golders Green underground station.

Hume led the way into the room and motioned for Setty to sit on the sofa, while he switched on the electric light and drew the curtains. It was about 6.30 in the evening.

'Where's your pretty wife, Donald?' enquired the big man, with a leer.

Hume felt the back of his neck getting hot. Although Setty hardly knew his wife, he had a way of referring to her which somehow hinted at a clandestine relationship. This was one of the many things about him which incensed Hume. Nevertheless he kept his voice calm.

'She's probably upstairs feeding the baby. Keep your voice down as she'll be wanting to get her off to sleep.'

Setty shrugged his heavy shoulders. 'I know you're short of money, Donald, what with the new baby and that, but I can't offer you any more commissions for cars. Not at the moment at any rate. The police have been nosing around again and I'll have to keep my nose clean, at least for a while.'

'I don't want any more car work, not for the moment. But I'll be disappointed if you're going to go all legal on me,' said Hume with a mock-reproachful look on his face.

'Well, I didn't say that,' put in Setty quickly. 'Not entirely, if you see what I mean? If you've got any suggestions?'

'Do you know where I can get hold of some war-surplus tommy guns and sten guns?'

'I might,' said Setty cautiously. 'What's in it for me?'

Hume sat down opposite the bulky man, crossed his legs casually and took out a silver cigarette-case from which he offered a cigarette to Setty. 'Why don't you buy some yourself?' said Hume. 'Act as middle-man to some people I know who want them overseas?'

'Overseas wouldn't be Palestine, would it?' asked Setty, taking a cigarette. 'We wouldn't be talking about flogging arms to the Israelis or the Arabs?'

'What if we were?'

The big man leaned forward so that the smaller Hume could light his cigarette. Then he sat back chortling. His wide chest and belly shook with mirth. 'You are a card, Donald. Did you know I was born in Baghdad? And I share a flat with my sister and her oh-so respectable husband, who also comes from the same part of the world. How do you think they would feel if they knew I was flogging guns which happened to end up with the Israelis?'

'You mean you're not interested?'

'I didn't say that, Donald,' continued Setty, still chuckling. 'It simply means that I should have to take a pretty big cut to salve my conscience!'

And with this he burst out laughing.

Small, pudgy-looking Hume could have cheerfully smashed him in the face there and then. The man's self-satisfied amusement raised the anger in him and he thought of all the things he hated about Setty.

He recalled a day not so long ago when he'd been in Setty's garage. Although the man did most of his car-dealing in Warren Street, he still kept a garage not far away in Cambridge Terrace Mews. Hume had with him his constant companion, his half-Alsatian half-Husky dog, Tony. Nearby stood a car which had been freshly resprayed. It had a window open and Tony, who had a habit of doing this, jumped in through the car window and scratched the new paint.

Setty had been furious. He had shouted at Hume to get his dog away and had viciously kicked the animal when it came close enough. This, in turn, had upset Hume. Kicking his dog was like kicking him. And in that moment he had vowed vengeance.

Now his moment had come. But he needed Setty in a relaxed frame of mind. Tonight he'd purposely left the dog in another room with the door shut, so that Setty should not see it. He forced a smile.

'I expected you'd want a large cut, Stanley. But provided you can supply the goods we can do a deal.'

'And how do you come into this, Donald?' said Setty in his insinuating manner, as if he couldn't imagine Hume being involved in anything so important as the sale of arms. Then realization appeared on his face. 'Oh yes, I know! They call you the Flying Smuggler, don't they? You're going to fly the guns out, aren't you?'

'You're too clever for me, Stanley,' said Hume from between stiff lips. 'You've guessed it. I'm going to fly a Halifax freighter, ostensibly empty of course, to Spain to pick up a load of fruit. When I get there the guns will be loaded into Spanish fruit-boats and shipped to Palestine.'

'Very clever,' said Setty, holding up the cigarette with its long column of ash and looking round irritably.

Hume jumped to his feet. 'I'll get you an ashtray.'

This was the moment he had been waiting for. The time when he would get back at the man from Baghdad – repay him for all his veiled insinuations, the small injuries to his vanity and for the kick Setty had aimed at his dog. But probably the main reason he had decided to despatch the big man, and on this particular day, was the nice wad of notes that Setty carried in the back trousers pocket of his expensive blue suit.

The moment had come, but he had to force his trembling legs to walk round the back of the settee.

Stooping behind the couch he felt under it and quickly brought out the coil of rope he had previously placed there. It was a length of window cord with a small loop fashioned at one end. When the other end was passed through it made a noose.

He had thought about this instant for days. All he had to do was to drop the noose over the unsuspecting Setty's head and pull hard on the snakelike cord. He could lean back and the noose would tighten inexorably around the man's neck. He would only have to hold it for a short time. Then Setty's struggles would cease and it would all be over. The quick silent kill.

For it had to be silent. The paper-thin walls of the flat would soon alert his neighbours. The headmaster and his wife who lived downstairs would surely hear any commotion in the flat above. And his wife, who was in the bedroom above, would come down if she heard a fight going on below her.

Donald Hume rose to his feet. Leaned forward with trembling hands. Dropped the noose over Setty's head. And pulled with all his might.

But things went wrong, right from the start. Far from its being easy to haul back on the cord, Hume found that the powerful Setty was pulling him. The bulky man heaved himself forward and Hume found himself being slammed against the sofa. But he kept tight hold of the cord. So long as he exerted pressure on it he knew that the big man would eventually weaken. But he discovered that he was being jerked from side to side as the big man thrashed about on the settee, trying to free himself from the cord which was biting ever deeper into his bull-like neck.

Hume, however, had forgotten to loop the end of the cord round his wrist and with one last despairing lunge Setty hurled himself away and the cord slipped through Hume's sweaty fingers. The big man was free.

But the effort to liberate himself had exhausted Setty and he was unable to capitalize on his success. He

remained lying on the sofa, and when Hume looked over
he saw that the big man's face was purple, and he was
grappling with only weak fingers at the cord, which had
disappeared into the folds of his thick neck.

Hume knew that all was not lost. In the corridor outside
hung a German SS dagger. A wicked weapon with an
eight-inch blade, razor-sharp on each of its cutting edges.
He rushed into the hall and grabbed it from the wall.

Back in the sitting-room Setty was trying to get up from
the couch. Without thinking, Hume swung the knife
underarm. There was a thud as the weapon hit the big
man in the chest and a surprised look came on to his face.
Hume swung again and again. He didn't know how many
times he had hit him – it turned out to be five – before the
large bulk heeled over, like some great liner turning over
for its final plunge to the sea bottom.

Donald Hume stood panting, and realizing for a
moment that he had done it, actually killed Setty.

Had anybody heard anything? He stood listening.
Would the people from below come pounding up the
stairs wanting to know what the noise had been about?
Would his wife come down to see what was going on? But
he could hear nothing from downstairs, and above his
wife was moving about normally. Incredibly it seemed
nobody had heard anything.

He looked at his watch and realized that the whole
episode, from Setty's entering the flat to his collapse on
the sofa, had occupied only a few minutes. He then
noticed that the knife blade was dripping blood on to the
carpet and that blood from Setty's wounds was seeping
through on to the settee. Seizing the bulky man by the legs
he eased him carefully on to the floor, then began
dragging him across the carpet.

In his dreams this had been the easy part. Drag the body
across the small hall and into the dining-room. Then
across that into the scullery. From there into the kitchen
and a coal cupboard which was at the farthest end of the

flat under the sloping roof. He could keep the body in that until he was ready to deal with it, since his wife never went into the cupboard for fear of mice.

In reality, dragging the body proved to be one of the most difficult parts of the operation. Setty's corpse was heavy and difficult to move and by the time he had pulled it into the dining-room he had to stop and rest. Sweat was pouring off him. But once he had passed through the dining-room the going became easier because the floors were now covered with linoleum and the body slid more easily over the smooth surface. Eventually, he rolled the corpse into the low coal cupboard and covered it with a piece of felt.

Now he had to clear up the mess on the floors. With a face flannel and a bowl of water he soon cleaned away the blood stains on the linoleum, but the carpets proved more difficult. He managed to clean the carpet in the dining-room, but the one in the sitting-room was heavily bloodstained. He washed off as much as he could, deciding that although he might temporarily hide the remaining stains from his wife with furniture he could not do it for long. The next day he would have to get it cleaned. He noticed that blood had seeped on to the bare floor surrounding the carpet and thought that this too could be disguised if the floor was restained.

Then he realized that he had forgotten one of the main reasons for the murder, the £1,000 now residing in Setty's trousers. Back he went to the coal cupboard. But there he had a shock. There was no bundle of notes in the back pocket of the trousers. Hurriedly he turned the body over and searched the jacket pockets.

There they were in the inside pocket. But with horror he saw that one of the knife thrusts had gone through the bundle, cutting many of the notes and causing nearly all of them to become bloodstained.

This was an utter disaster. He couldn't wash and dry the notes without either his wife or the cleaning lady, who would be coming the next day, noticing them. The only thing he could do was to look carefully through the slashed bundle and extract the undamaged and unstained notes. Some, which were only a little bloody at the edges, he was able to salvage by snipping off the stained portions, and in this way he amassed a total of just over a £100, a far cry from the £1,000 he had been expecting.

There was one last thing he had to do that day: remove Setty's car, a Citroën, parked round the corner. Taking the key from the big man's pocket he picked up a coat and a pair of gloves and went downstairs. He had been careful to wear gloves earlier that evening when he had ridden with Setty from the drinking club where they had met, and he would have to be careful to wear them again when he got rid of the car. There must be no fingerprints linking him with the vehicle.

He drove the Citroën to Cambridge Terrace Mews, where Setty normally kept it, and left it outside the lock-up garage. Then, walking a few streets further away, he took a taxi home.

The next morning while his wife was upstairs, busy with their baby daughter, he moved the furniture in the lounge and rolled up the light green carpet which had been heavily stained with blood. Then, carrying it over his shoulder, he took it next door to a carpet cleaner's. Without unrolling it he asked for it to be cleaned and restained a darker green. Next he went to the bank to deposit the notes he had managed to save from the bloodstained bundle.

He could do no more about the body in the cupboard for the time being. His wife was going to take the baby to the children's hospital at Great Ormond Street that afternoon, which would give him the opportunity to deal with it. Mrs Stride, the cleaner, was due at half-past two, but with luck he would have completed his task by then. He was on tenterhooks until he heard the front door close behind his wife and child. It was then not quite one o'clock. An hour and a half before Mrs Stride was to arrive.

Hume had made up his mind long ago what he was going to do with Setty's body. It was far too big for him to manhandle down the stairs and out of the flat on his own. He would therefore have to cut it up. He had previously obtained a sharp linoleum knife and a hacksaw and had also collected some pieces of felt and an old grey blanket to help wrap up the dismembered body into parcels. Some heavy chunks of rubble from the back garden and some lead weights would help to weigh the parcels down when he got rid of them. For he was going to dump them where they would never be found – at the bottom of the sea.

Cutting off the legs proved quicker than he had expected as the hacksaw blade went through the thigh bones very easily.

He turned to the head. But as he took up the knife the sightless eyes of the dead man gazed up at him. Hume's hand shook and he had to turn his own head away. It took several minutes before he was able to control his shaking arm. Then he put a piece of cloth across those accusing eyes, and began again.

He had already selected a cardboard box to put the head in, one which he had obtained from the grocer downstairs and which had previously contained tins of baked beans. And with the head packed in, surrounded by pieces of rubble, he carefully made a parcel of the box.

But that was as far as he could go. The effort had unnerved and exhausted him and he contented himself with wrapping the remaining torso in the felt and blanket and tying lead weights around it. Then, stuffing the various packages back into the coal cupboard, he cleaned up the mess in the kitchen.

During all this time his dog Tony had been confined in another room. Now he was let out and accompanied his master downstairs. Hume was carrying the parcel containing the legs under his right arm and the box containing the head under his left. In his raincoat pocket he carried the SS dagger, the lino knife and the dismantled hacksaw wrapped in paper. Halfway down the stairs he met the cleaning lady, who was coming up.

'Just taking some parcels to post, Mrs Stride. See you later this afternoon.'

Downstairs, Hume carried his parcels through the back garden and out into a lane that ran behind the houses. Here he had parked a black Singer car which he had hired. Loading the parcels into the back seat and the dog into the front, Hume drove round into Finchley Road.

He was making for Elstree, an airport to the north-west of London, some eight miles from Golders Green, where he was well known. In 1948 he had joined and taken lessons at the United Services Flying Club there, and obtained his civilian 'C' pilot's licence. When he arrived and asked to hire a light plane for a flight to Southend he was supplied with a single-engine Auster, licence plate G-AGXT.

He drove the car to where the plane was parked and loaded the parcels into it.

'No. You're not coming this time, Tony old chap – back into the car.'

He left the dog looking at him sorrowfully through the car window, climbed into the aircraft and soon the little blue Auster was flying in the direction of Southend. It was just after three o'clock, 2½ hours to sunset.

According to Hume's later account of the flight he swung south, crossed the South Coast and turned west to fly up the Channel to a position north of Sark in the Channel Islands. This, however, would be a journey of well over 200 miles and with the Auster's cruising speed of 70 m.p.h. would have taken not less than three hours; whereas, in fact, he landed at Southend by 6.15 p.m. It is much more likely, since Hume was hopeless at navigation, that he simply flew east, crossing the coast at Southend and flying on over the North Sea.

Having decided that he was far enough from land, he opened the aircraft door and one by one threw out the dagger, lino knife and hacksaw, followed by the two parcels. He looked for signs of them on the sea surface, but could see none. They had vanished completely. He turned for home.

Daylight had nearly gone by the time he landed at Southend. This meant that he was unable to fly on to Elstree, since his licence did not allow him to fly at night. Leaving the Auster with instructions that it should be refuelled and saying that he would collect it the next day, he took a taxi back to London. He put through a telephone call to Elstree to ask the ground staff there to take his dog out for a run and then allow the animal to sleep in the car.

The next day he called a local decorator and asked him to come and restain the edges of the sitting-room and dining-room floors, then went to Elstree to pick up the hired car and Tony.

Back again at the flat he investigated the coal cupboard. He had one final parcel to remove and drop in the sea, and then the job was finished.

But this final package proved to be a problem. The size of it and the lead weights he'd tied to the outside made it awkward to handle and very heavy. As he wrestled it out of the cupboard he realized that he would never be able to carry it downstairs without assistance.

He went into the sitting-room where the decorator was working.

'I wonder if you'd give me a hand with a heavy parcel?'

'Certainly, sir,' said the man and followed Hume into the kitchen. 'Is this it?' He pointed at the grey bundle, then bent to get his hands underneath.

At that moment Hume saw a dark stain beginning to seep through on the underside of the grey blanket.

'No,' he said quickly. 'Don't put your hands underneath. It'll be easier to lift by the cords.'

The man obediently straightened and took hold of the cords at one end while Hume got a grip on the other. They struggled to lift it.

'My God,' said the man. 'What have you got in it – a body?' Then he laughed.

Donald Hume responded with a weak smile.

They managed, by a process of lifting and sliding, to get the package to the top of the stairs. But, as it bumped and jostled down the steps, Hume was conscious that the parcel was making ominous gurgling noises.

'What on earth have you got in there?' enquired the decorator.

'Fish,' said Hume.

Eventually they succeeded in getting the parcel out of the front door of the flat, across the pavement and into the front passenger seat of the Singer Hume had parked in Finchley Road. This time Tony had to go in the back.

Hume drove to Southend Airport. He positioned his car as close to the small aircraft as he could and with great difficulty hoisted the bulky object on to the ground. Out of the corner of his eye he could see a member of the ground staff approaching. He didn't want the man to get near enough to become suspicious of the bundle or to start asking awkward questions, so with a superhuman effort he heaved it up and rammed it through the open door of the aircraft and on to the passenger seat.

The groundstaff employee stopped in his tracks. 'I was going to ask you if you wanted a hand with that.'

'No thanks,' sang out Hume cheerily. 'Thanks all the same.'

He was soon away again, this time with the faithful Tony in the seat behind the pilot. He flew on the same course as the day before, and when he judged he had cleared the coast by a sufficient amount, throttled back and leaned over to release the door catch.

He pushed the bulky bundle beside him, but it did not move. He gripped the control column with his knees to leave his hands free then got both of them behind the package and heaved. Nothing happened. The large parcel remained solidly in the seat beside him.

For one crazy moment he imagined that Setty had come back to life and was sitting there defying him. Then he wiped the sweat from his face and took control of himself.

He banked the plane steeply. The bundle slid down against the door, but there it stuck. He heaved against it once again. Still it wouldn't move. By this time his tension had communicated itself to the dog which was barking furiously. Above the roar of the engine he shouted for the animal to keep quiet; then realized that should the door open quickly with the plane canted over the dog might fall out as well.

He grabbed Tony's collar with one hand while pushing at the bundle with the other, still keeping the control column gripped between his knees. But through the windscreen he saw the horizon move up and knew that not only were they banking, but they were nose-diving towards the sea.

Suddenly there was a loud bang and the small plane jerked up momentarily. Hume saw that the bundle had gone. Then there was another bang as the slip-stream caught the door and crashed it shut. He let out a sigh of relief and gripped the control column with his hands to pull the aircraft out of its dive.

He could hear a clattering and banging from behind and looking round was horrified to see that the outer covering of the parcel, the grey blanket with the lead weights attached, had become detached and was now flapping and banging on the tail plane of the little aircraft.

Then, just as suddenly as it had started, the noise ceased and he saw that the blanket was now gone.

But the damage had been done. With a sinking heart he banked round to circle the spot where the bundle had gone down. And there, far below, but bobbing about defiantly on the surface of the sea, was the felt-covered torso.

The thrusting and shoving of the bundle through the door of the little plane must have loosened the outer

covering, the grey blanket and the weights. And without
these it would not sink.

This looked like the end of his perfect murder. If the torso
did not sink there was a strong possibility it would be
washed up somewhere or even spotted by some passing
ship and picked up. And the police, having something to
work on, might – just possibly might – trace the murder
back to him.

It was a harrowing thought and for a moment he
entertained a wild idea of bringing down the aircraft in the
sea near the torso, tying it to the plane and allowing them
both to sink together while he swam ashore. But he was a
long way from land and didn't know if he could swim that
far. Better to risk the bundle being discovered. It would still
be very difficult for the police to connect him with the body,
even if they did discover whose it was. He set a course for
Elstree.

As Hume came in over the Kent coast he became aware
that he was hopelessly lost. He landed in a field and
discovered that he was not far from Faversham. It was now
getting dark and he knew he could not get back to Elstree
that night, so he took off and made for Gravesend Airport,
landing there at 6.30 p.m. He had to hire another car to take
him and Tony back to London, but he still had a few of
Setty's fivers left.

The following day he collected the car from Elstree
Airport and began his anxious vigil of watching the papers
for any news of the torso's being washed ashore.

There was plenty of news about the disappearance of
Setty, for his brother-in-law had reported him missing
when he didn't come home that first night. And the
newspapers soon got hold of the story. He became known
as 'The Man with the Fivers', and theories as to what had
happened to him soon filled the columns.

Hume read them all with anxiety, but his apprehension
gradually eased as the days went by and there was no hard
news of Setty. He began to think that he had got away with

it after all.

But on Sunday, 23 October, he opened the *Sunday Pictorial* and saw the banner headlines, 'SETTY TORSO WASHED UP'. And Donald Hume's world came crashing down around him.

The body had been discovered the previous Friday, by Mr Sidney Tiffin, a farm worker. He had gone out that morning to shoot wild fowl in his punt on the marshes bordering Blackwater River, near the village of Tillingham in Essex. Seeing the grey bundle floating in the stream he had at first ignored it, then thought that it might be one of the RAF training drogues and if so would be worth some money if he recovered it. But after opening the parcel and discovering what it was, he carefully tied it to a pole, so that it would not be washed out to sea again on the ebbing tide, and went in search of the local police.

The torso was removed to St John's Hospital mortuary at Chelmsford and Superintendent G.H. Totterdell of the Essex County CID got in touch with Dr Francis E. Camps, professor of Forensic Medicine at the University of London, and Home Office pathologist, who came to Chelmsford to perform the post-mortem.

During the examination Superintendent Totterdell remarked to Dr Camps, 'I think we've got Setty's body here.'

'Very likely,' said the pathologist. 'If I remove a sample of skin from the hands, Fred Cherrill at the Yard might be able to confirm it.'

He made an incision round the wrists and was able to peel off the entire skin of the hands like a pair of gloves. Totterdell then took the samples to Chief Superintendent Fred Cherrill, Scotland Yard's fingerprint expert.

Up to that time it had been extremely difficult to get fingerprints from bodies which had been in the water for more than a few days. But Cherrill developed a new technique with the skin from Setty's fingers. By treating them with a special solution and sticking portions of the

skin on to the fingers of rubber gloves he wore himself he
was able to get satisfactory prints.

Setty's fingerprints were on file, for he had served a
term of eighteen months in 1926 for offences under the
Bankruptcy Acts. And they matched with those of the
torso found on the Essex marshes.

At 7.30 a.m. on the morning of Thursday, 27 October,
only six days after the discovery of the torso, police
officers knocked at the door of Donald Hume's flat. Led by
Chief Inspector Jamieson and Detective Inspector Evan
Davies, they escorted Hume to Albany Street police
station.

He was told that enquiries were being made in
connection with the murder of Stanley Setty and it was
thought that he might be able to help them.

'No, I'm afraid I can't help you with that,' said Hume. 'I
know nothing about it.'

The police were very nice to him. They gave him cups of
tea and cigarettes. Then the questioning was taken over by
Superintendent Colin MacDougall, who was in charge of
the investigation, and his assistant Sergeant Neil
Sutherland.

'You know,' said the superintendent conversationally,
'Dr Camps, who conducted the post-mortem on Setty, is a
very clever fellow. During the war he would sometimes be
called upon to do PMs on people who had fallen out of
aeroplanes and landed without a parachute, and he
recognized the same type of injuries on the torso of Setty.
We looked at first for a cliff he might have been thrown
off, but there wasn't one near enough to where the body
was found. Then we thought of an aeroplane itself.

'It was easy after that. We made enquiries at local
aerodromes and heard about this chap who'd taken off
from Elstree the day after Setty disappeared with a couple
of heavy parcels, and who was seen to land at Southend a
couple of hours later – with no parcels in the plane at all.
Then the next day he took off from Southend with a very

heavy parcel – he refused an offer of help with it – and subsequently landed at Gravesend, again with no parcel remaining in the plane. Curious, isn't it? For that man was you, Mr Hume! And we have no end of witnesses who will swear it was.'

Hume licked his lips. 'Doesn't prove that the parcels were Setty.'

'No? Well how about this then? Setty had over a £1,000 in five-pound notes on him when he disappeared. But what you didn't realize when you killed him and stole the money was that he'd only got it from the bank that very day. The numbers of the notes were consecutive, and the bank has a record of them! So the five-pound note you gave for the hire of a car to take you to Golders Green from Southend we traced as being from the lot that Setty had. And the notes you paid into the bank the next day all came from Setty as well. How do you explain that?'

Hume dropped his face into his hands. And when he raised it his eyes were streaming with tears.

'I'm several kinds of bastard, aren't I?'

Superintendent MacDougall looked at him for a moment then said: 'Perhaps you'd better tell us all about it.'

Hume sniffed a bit, wiped his eyes and began his story. 'Some time ago, I met a man called Mac. He introduced me to a man who was known as Greeny. They offered me money to drop some parcels from a plane.

'On October 5th, Mac and Greeny called at my flat with another man they called "Boy". Greeny and Boy each carried a parcel. Mac told me that they had been making forged petrol coupons and wanted to get rid of the plates and presses by dumping them in the sea. They all had large bundles of notes and Boy gave me ten five-pound notes as payment.

Hume then went on to describe dropping the two parcels from the aircraft.

When he returned, Mac was waiting on the pavement

just outside the front door and took him across to a large
Humber car at the kerb. He noticed another bulky package
on the back seat. Eventually, after some argument, it was
arranged that he would keep the parcel in his flat overnight
and drop it the following day.

'They paid me £90 in fivers and £10 in pound notes and
then Mac and the Boy carried the big parcel up to my flat
and stowed it in the coal cupboard. I asked them what was
in it and they said "the same as before".

'When they'd gone I moved the parcel to one side of the
cupboard. It made a kind of gurgling noise and I saw there
was a pool of blood where it'd been. That frightened me.
Then I noticed blood on the floor of the dining-room where
the parcel had rested and I quickly wiped it up with the first
cloth that came to hand.'

Hume related how the next morning his wife had left to
take the child to the hospital and he dragged the parcel out
into the kitchen.

'I picked it up and started to walk through the dining-
room, but then I dropped it and it squirted blood. I dragged
it into the hall, then went and got another piece of material,
I think it was one of my wife's old dresses torn up, and
tucked it in around the parcel.'

He then told the story of how the decorator helped him
carry the parcel downstairs and how he had taken it to
Southend and subsequently dropped it in the sea.

When he was asked why he didn't go to the police when
he suspected he was getting rid of a body, he replied that he
didn't think they would believe him. 'They haven't time for
shady characters like me.'

Not surprisingly, the police did not believe this incredible
story and Donald Hume was sent for trial at the Old Bailey,
on 18 January 1950, on a charge of murdering Stanley Setty,
and of being an accessory after the fact to murder. Mr Justice
Lewis presided and the prosecution was conducted by Mr
Christmas Humphreys, Senior Treasury Counsel. The
defence was in the hands of Mr R.F. Levy.

During the night, after the first day of the trial, the judge was taken seriously ill and was replaced the next day by Mr Justice Sellers. The trial was restarted with the new judge and a fresh jury.

On the face of it the prosecution had a strong case. There was a large bloodstain on the back of Hume's sitting-room carpet and traces of blood between the cracks of the floorboards in the dining-room. Blood had even soaked into the lath and plaster of the ceiling beneath and there was more on the edge of the green lino in the hall. Where there was enough blood to be typed it was found to correspond to Setty's blood group.

The police searched long and hard to find Mac, Green and the Boy. Warren Street and its environs were carefully searched and the whole country was canvassed. But no trace of them could be found.

On the other hand, Hume's story, although incredible, was just possible, and it did explain the bloodstains, the five-pound notes and the flights with the parcels.

It all depended on whether the jury would believe Hume or not. In the witness-box he was calm and confident and very plausible. Under cross-examination he stood up well to Mr Humphreys, snapping back answers as quickly as the questions were put, and he could not be tripped up. He clearly impressed the jury.

In his summing-up, however, Mr Justice Sellers – redressing the balance a little – clearly pointed to the incredible nature of Hume's story. The jury, after retiring for 2½ hours, returned to state that they were hopelessly divided and that there was no possibility of their agreeing a verdict.

Mr Christmas Humphreys then said that he did not feel the interests of justice would be served by a new trial. He would therefore call no evidence on the murder charge, but would offer evidence on the second indictment, that of being an accessory after the fact.

Before a new jury Hume was found not guilty of murder

and thus escaped the hangman. To the next charge, Hume had already admitted helping to dispose of Setty's body, and he therefore pleaded guilty to being an accessory.

Mr Justice Sellers sentenced him to twelve years' imprisonment.

Hume served eight years, earning a full remission for good conduct, and was released from prison on 1 February 1958. In April he changed his name by deed poll to Donald Brown and during May he sold his story to the *Sunday Pictorial*. It included a full confession to the murder and his story ran in a series of articles during the month of June.

In his confession he said that he found Setty waiting for him at his flat when he arrived home on the evening of 4 October. There was bad feeling between them and an argument developed. He claimed that he got the German SS dagger off the wall merely to frighten Setty into leaving, but the man taunted him and swung at him with the back of his hand. A fight developed and they rolled on the floor. Hume stabbed him repeatedly in the chest and legs and eventually Setty collapsed on the floor and died there.

This is plainly at variance with the facts. It was brought out by the defence at the trial that a rough-and-tumble fight on the floor would almost certainly have been heard by other members of the house.

In addition, if Setty was attacked from the front in the way Hume describes, he would surely have sustained injures to the hands and arms as he tried to protect himself. This was maintained by Dr Robert Donald Teare, a well-known pathologist called by the defence. Setty had no such injuries.

Although it is fairly certain that Hume did murder Setty he almost certainly did not do it as he claimed. It is much more likely that it was a planned killing in the way I have described at the beginning of this chapter.

Hume left the country before his confession appeared in

the newspaper, although he could not have been tried again for the murder. With £2,000 in his pockets he flew to Switzerland.

In 1951, he had been divorced by his wife on the grounds of cruelty, but in Zurich he soon found himself a girlfriend. Trudi Sommer was in her late twenties, had been divorced and now ran a hairdressing establishment in the city.

Hume soon ran through the money he had obtained for his story and then, in marked contrast to the planning and resourcefulness he had shown during the murder of Setty, began a series of crude bank robberies. Using Zurich as a base, he travelled to England under assumed names and undertook two raids, both at the Midland Bank in Brentford, near London.

On the first occasion, in August 1959, he walked into the bank waving a gun, shot a cashier in the stomach, and got away with £1,300. When he repeated the procedure in the following November, this time at the bank's new premises, he shot and severely wounded the branch manager, but netted only £300.

The following January he raided the Gewerbe Bank in Zurich. Placing his gun in a cardboard box he walked into the bank at 11.30 a.m. one Friday morning. Setting the box on the counter he fired at one of the cashiers, wounding him, and leaped over the counter to grab as much money as he could. But the wounded man set off the alarm and another clerk struggled with him. Hume threw him off and raced out into the street. He was pursued by two bank clerks and some passers-by. Several times he turned to fire at the crowd following, but his gun jammed. He fled into a small square where there was a taxi rank. One of the taxi drivers, sizing up the situation, jumped at the quarry.

Hume shot him at point-blank range and the man collapsed. Hume was soon afterwards captured by the crowd and only the speedy arrival of the police prevented him suffering serious injury at the hands of the angry mob. The taxi driver died in the street a few minutes later.

Hume was charged with murder.

He was brought to trial on 24 September 1959 at Winterthur, near Zurich, only one year and eight months after being released from prison in England. He was found guilty and sentenced to imprisonment with hard labour for life. As he was being taken away he kicked out at a photographer and fought with his guards.

He began his prison sentence by being reasonably co-operative and was allowed to receive visits and parcels from the faithful Trudi. As time went on he became increasingly violent and spent long periods in solitary confinement. In 1970, after eleven years of imprisonment, the Swiss authorities complained that they could no longer cope with him, as he had developed schizophrenic tendencies, but it was only after sixteen years of imprisonment that he was finally returned to Britain. He was transferred to Broadmoor, where he still remains.

2   Harold Loughans:
Underground Alibi

From downstairs there came the sudden sound of breaking glass. Mrs Rose Ada Robinson sat up in bed with a jerk. A 63-year-old widow, she lived by herself, above the John Barleycorn public house in Commercial Road, Portsmouth, and she was in constant fear of being burgled.

She shivered and clutched the bedclothes more tightly around her. It might be someone breaking glass outside, for her small bedroom overlooked the back yard of the pub. On the other hand it might be someone breaking the bar parlour window downstairs.

She clutched her two bags to her chest. One was a lady's handbag containing banknotes neatly rolled up and secured by elastic bands. The other was a leather hold-all containing coins: half crowns and two-shilling pieces, shillings and sixpences and so on. This money was the takings from the pub's tills. And since it was her custom to pay the cash in to the brewery once a month, and this was the early morning of Monday, 29 November, she had nearly a month's takings in the bags. Altogether about £400: a considerable sum of money in 1943.

She heard a creak on the stairs and a cold feeling gripped her stomach. She began to tremble. Her worst fears were confirmed. There was someone in the house.

Sliding the bags down under the sheets, she gripped the edge of the bedclothes. She would lie quietly and hope that the intruder would go away. With the roller-blind black-out up at the window it was pitch dark in the room and there was a chance that whoever looked in might think that it was unoccupied. She held her breath.

Then a thought struck her. If she could reach the window she might pull the blackout aside and shout for help. There were plenty of people nearby. A naval stoker was home on leave next door. And she knew that a man would be on duty fire-watching, in a factory just at the back. Her right hand moved cautiously across her body, gripping the bedclothes in preparation for flinging them back quickly.

A light from a torch suddenly shone on her face, momentarily blinding her.

'Who are you?' she quavered. 'What do you want?'

The man behind the torch didn't answer.

At 8 a.m. the same morning the charlady, Mrs Eva Firman, arrived outside the front door of the John Barleycorn. After knocking for some time and getting no reply she hammered on the front door of the next house. Eventually a bleary-eyed young man came to the door. He was William Stevens, the young sailor. On hearing Mrs Firman's plight he obligingly went through his own house to the back and climbed over the wall separating his yard from that of the John Barleycorn. He found the back door of the pub wide open. Walking along the downstairs passage he opened the front door to the charlady.

'I don't like the look of it, Mrs Firman. The back door was open and somebody's smashed the bar parlour window. I think there's been a burglary. We ought to get in touch with the police.'

'Don't you think we ought to call Mrs Robinson first?'

The young man nodded and they both went upstairs. They discovered Mrs Robinson in the small bedroom at the rear, lying on her back on the floor. She was partially clothed because she never undressed fully when she went to bed, beause of the air raids. A blue cloth covered her face and chest. She was dead.

The police were informed and Superintendent F. Fuggle and Inspector Lamport of the Portsmouth CID arrived and took charge of the investigation. A detailed search of the premises was begun, including a hunt for fingerprints, and a start was made interviewing neighbours who might have heard or seen something suspicious during the night.

The following day Dr Keith Simpson, the Home Office pathologist, visited the scene of the crime and later made a post-mortem examination. He was then able to reconstruct the crime. He suggested that Mrs Robinson had made a dive for the window before she was grabbed. The roller blind had come down and there was a bruise on her head showing where she had collided with the window-sill. Then she had been pulled back and down on the floor. When she was on her back someone had knelt or sat astride her and strangled her.

There was a deep bruise on one side of her neck, possibly made by a thumb, and three more bruises in a line with the first – obviously the marks of the fingers of someone's right hand. But there were no curved fingernail impressions. Dr Simpson put the time of death at between two and four o'clock on the Monday morning.

This was later confirmed by the police investigation. Two doors along another woman had been awoken the same night by banging on her kitchen window at the back. She used to sleep with her little boy in the front room on the ground floor because of the bombing. She heard the blackout being knocked down in the kitchen, then heavy footsteps outside her door. But they didn't come into her room and eventually went away.

After some time she heard footfalls along the passage adjoining her house and looking out of the front window she saw a motor car between her house and the John Barleycorn and four men standing nearby. The time was just before three o'clock.

The police assumed that the robbers had first broken into the house thinking it was the John Barleycorn, but realizing their mistake had left without stealing anything, and had gone on to the pub.

The murder room at the John Barleycorn was in a shambles. All the drawers of the dressing-table had been taken out and their contents scattered about the floor. The bed was in disarray, with all the clothes mixed up with the green eiderdown. Several mats were strewn about on the floor as if a desperate struggle had taken place. The two bags which had contained the money were on the top of the dressing-table, but they were empty.

Downtairs the picture was clearer. The broken sash window plainly indicated the method of entry, and the robbers had left by unbolting the back door. But there were no usable fingerprints anywhere, and the only thing the burglars had left behind was a small black button on the sill just below the broken window. Attached to it was a small piece of thread. It was the sort of button which could have come from the cuff of a coat.

Apart from this the police had few clues to go on, and it soon became obvious that the investigation was completely bogged down. But then, three weeks later, an incident occurred which changed the whole complexion of the case.

At about 4.30 p.m. on Tuesday, 21 December, Angus Maclean and Herbert Baker of the Metropolitan Police were walking in plain clothes along Waterloo Road in London. They saw a short, thickset man with a parcel under his arm, looking round nervously and generally acting in a suspicious manner. He entered the Anchor Café and they followed him in.

He went up to the counter and unwrapped the parcel.

'Know anybody who wants to buy a new pair of boots

for twenty-five bob, love?' he said in a Yorkshire accent to the woman behind the counter.

The two policemen appeared, one on either side of the small man.

'I wonder if you'd care to explain how you came by those boots?'

The man looked up at the two burly policemen. 'If it's any business of yours, my brother sent them to me for Christmas. But they're much too big for me.'

'I'm not satisfied with that explanation,' said one. 'I think you're in possession of stolen property. Perhaps you'd better come along with us.'

They took him to the police box on Waterloo Road and phoned for a black maria. They cautioned him, but he proved to be a very voluble talker.

'I'm wanted for much more serious crimes than pinching some boots,' he gabbled. 'Scotland Yard are after me,' he said proudly. Then his face became sad. 'It's the trapdoor for me now.'

He seemed to have a mercurial personality and his behaviour astonished the constables, but they let him prattle on. 'I'm glad you've brought me in,' he said when he arrived at the police station. 'I've been in hell these last few weeks. I didn't mean to kill her, but I had to stop her screaming. You know what it is when a woman screams.'

Then he began to cry. Through his sobs the policemen heard him say: 'I know this is the end of the road for me. I want to say I done the murder job in Hampshire about fourteen days ago.'

At nine o'clock that night he was interviewed by Detective Sergeant Clark of the Metropolitan Police and the small man agreed to make a formal statement. By that time the police had discovered that his name was Harold Loughans, an old lag, who had spent twenty-eight of his forty-seven years in prison.

In his statement he said that around the end of November he'd been to Portsmouth and had a drink in a

pub the name of which he couldn't remember. In the bar
he got talking to a regular who told him that the landlady,
who lived alone, kept about £2,000 on the premises. He
thought the matter over and, later that day when the pub
was closed, went round the back, climbed over a wall and
got in through a window. He was searching in a room for
the money when a woman of about sixty entered. He
grabbed her and told her to keep quiet. But she screamed
and he put his hands round her throat. She went quiet
and he thought she had fainted, so he left her lying on the
floor. He found a lot of money, mostly five-pound notes
tied up with string, in a little desk. He didn't intend to kill
her, only to stop her screaming.

The Portsmouth police had been told of Loughans's
arrest and just after midnight, Inspector Lamport and
Sergeant Atkins arrived at the Kennington Road police
station. Inspector Lamport was shown Loughans's
statement and he shook his head.

'It doesn't bear much relation to the facts. The pub was
the John Barleycorn and although the burglar did get in
through a back window he didn't get money from a little
desk. There wasn't one there.'

'He was right about strangling the old lady, though,
wasn't he?' asked Detective Sergeant Clark.

Inspector Lamport shook his head again. 'According to
the post-mortem she was strangled with one hand only,
the right.'

'Well, I think that puts Loughans right out of it. When
you see him take a look at his right hand. He's got no
fingers on it. Lost them in an accident in his youth, he
says. I don't think he could strangle anyone with it.'

The inspector went to see Loughans and read the man's
statement to him aloud. Then he said: 'Is all this true?'

'Of course it's all true. Don't you think I did it?'

'In some areas the statement differs from what we know
to be the facts,' said the inspector cautiously.

'Oh, I've done so many jobs lately I can't keep track of

them all. Last week I broke into a house in St Albans, tied an old woman to a bed and robbed her.'

'What about the John Barleycorn job?'

Loughans thought about it for a while. 'When I got upstairs in the public-house I saw a woman in the back bedroom. She screamed and I caught her by the throat. She fell down near the window and banged her head on the floor and the blackout came down as well. I thought she'd fainted. She looked so awful I covered her face with a piece of cloth. Did she have a bad heart? She went out so quickly. I took some money out of some bags and got out of there as quick as I could.'

'Will you make another statement?'

'No, I'm too tired. If you're going to take me back to Pompey let me have a sleep on the way down, then I'll tell you all about it.'

'Show me your right hand.'

The small man raised his mutilated hand. He still had his thumb, but had lost the rest of his fingers down to the second joint. 'Did that when I was fourteen. Got it caught in a machine in a brickyard.'

They went to Portsmouth by car, with Loughans sleeping most of the way, and when they arrived at Fratton police station he again asked if he could have a sleep. After this he was ready to make another statement.

This second statement was much longer than the first and was substantially the same story he had told Inspector Lamport at the Kennington Road Police Station. It did contain some additional information, such as the fact that the dressing-table in Mrs Robinson's bedroom had a glass top – which it had. And that the old lady wore no rings – which was also correct.

He also volunteered the information that he had passed the money on to a woman confederate who had instructions to go away if Loughans was ever arrested. But he refused to give away any more about her or the man who had driven the car.

The inspector produced some more clothes for Loughans
to wear and when the small man had removed his jacket
the policeman looked carefully at the cuffs. Loughans
grinned when he saw the inspector examining the coat.
'You won't find any evidence there, I'm afraid. After I
done the job I found a button missing, so when I got back
to London I pulled them all off.'

Loughans's clothes were then examined at the
Metropolican Police laboratory at Hendon.

Sometime later the inspector conferred with his
superior, Detective Superintendent Fuggle.

'The report from Hendon has just come in,' said the
superintendent. 'The hair on the handbag was quite
unlike Loughans's, obviously some of Mrs Robinson's.'
He turned a page. 'Then of the hairs and fibres removed
from Loughans's clothing, only three, from his boots and
trouser turn-ups, corresponded to the material of the mats
from Mrs Robinson's bedroom floor.'

'Well, I suppose that's something,' said the inspector.

The superintendent shook his head. 'All you can say is
that those three fibres could have come from the bedroom
floor. Not that they definitely did.' He flicked over some
more pages. 'There was also a small piece of feather which
could have come from the eiderdown on the bed.'

'But also, I suppose, from many other eiderdowns?'

'Exactly,' muttered the superintendent. 'The button and
thread, now. That's a bit more hopeful. Although
Loughans had cut all the cuff buttons off, we still managed
to find some small pieces of thread left. There were some
in the tuck of the left sleeve. And they were similar to the
thread still attached to the button, and also to some which
had been used to sew on two buttons on the front of the
coat. Mind you, the other buttons on Loughans's coat
were sewn on with different thread.'

'Not very conclusive,' remarked the inspector.

'We've a bit more positive news from Dr Simpson,'
continued the superintendent. 'As you know, we took

some photographs and had a plaster cast made of Loughans's hand, which we sent on to Dr Simpson. Well, he's definitely of the opinion that Loughans could have strangled the old lady with that hand. Dr Simpson claims that with those short stumps Loughans can exert more force than a normal man can with all his fingers. And he's prepared to go into court and say so!'

'That's very good news.'

'Yes it is,' agreed the superintendent. He sat back in his chair and looked across the desk. 'What's your opinion of him, inspector?' he asked. 'You've seen more of him than anyone else here.'

The inspector scratched his chin. 'He's a very unstable character, of that there is no doubt. One minute he's up in the air, the next he's down in the dumps. But he's a chatterbox, sir, you can't stop him talking. And he craves attention. He'd do anything to get himself noticed.'

'That's what I was wondering. Do you really believe his confession?'

'Well, it's very detailed,' said the inspector cautiously. 'He knows a great deal about the murder that's not available to the general public. He must have got his information from somewhere.'

'Exactly, inspector. But can we be quite sure that he got it because he was there? Don't forget we have a witness who saw four men and a car outside the John Barleycorn. What if Loughans was only one of the four, perhaps not even the one who went inside? Or perhaps he simply has a confederate who was there and told him all about it?'

'He is an inveterate liar, sir. I grant you that.'

'I'll tell you why I asked your opinion of him. Did you know that two or three years ago he told the Stafford police that he had committed a murder in Scotland? And it was shown afterwards that he couldn't possibly have done it?'

The inspector nodded his head. 'I can well believe it, sir.'

The superintendent was silent for some time. 'The Director of Public Prosecutions thinks that we've enough evidence to go ahead and charge him with murder. But … I'm still not happy about it.'

The policeman's misgivings were amply justified a few weeks later when Loughans applied to see the governor of the prison in which he was being held and declared that he was innocent of the charge of murder. He claimed that his so-called confessions were lies and the result of the police's prompting him and putting words in his mouth. When he next appeared in court on remand he asked, for the first time, for legal aid and said: 'I'm not guilty of this charge, and I can prove it.' And as it turned out this was no idle boast.

The trial opened on Monday, 6 March 1944 at the Hampshire Assizes in Winchester, before Mr Justice Atkinson. Mr J.D. Casswell, KC, prosecuted and Loughans was defended by Mr J. Maude, KC.

Although the prosecution apparently had a strong case it depended almost entirely on Loughans's confessions. No one had seen him near the scene of the crime at the time of the murder. The forensic evidence against him was very inconclusive and the money had not been traced back to him or even recovered.

In his opening speech for the defence Mr John Maude conceded that Loughans was a liar. A man who lived in a fantasy world. He also admitted that the prisoner was a burglar. But he was not, he claimed, a murderer. Then he sprang his surprise.

Loughans had an alibi. During the night and early morning of Sunday and Monday, when the murder had been committed, Loughans had been seen at Warren Street underground station in London by four witnesses.

Even that late in the war, people in London still used the underground stations, when the trains had stopped running, as air-raid shelters. Bunks had been set up on the platforms and people who lived in the area would frequently sleep there.

Mr Maude called Mrs Edna Costors. She was a married woman with a baby and she lived in Gower Street, near Warren Street.

'Now, Mrs Costors, will you tell the court when you first saw the prisoner?'

'Yes, I remember him sitting on a bunk.'

'What time would that be?'

'That would be about five to nine on Sunday, 28 November.'

'What happened when you saw the prisoner?'

'He spoke to me about my baby, who had been crying, and asked me if he could hold her.'

'Did you notice anything about him?'

'Yes, when he was nursing her, I noticed that he had some fingers missing from his right hand.'

'And did he say anything else?'

'Yes. He said he came from Huddersfield. The British Legion had sent him to London for some light work and he was going to start in a hotel the next morning. He asked me if he could spend the night in the shelter and I said yes.'

She then described how at about eleven o'clock her two friends arrived and they all talked together, including Loughans. They turned in for the night at about half-past twelve and Loughans slept two bunks away.

'Now, Mrs Costors, did you see the prisoner after that?'

'Yes. I had to get up at five minutes to three in the morning and I passed his bunk. The old raincoat he had over him had slid off his feet and I pulled it back.' And she went on to relate how she had called him in the morning.

Her story was confirmed by her two friends, Rachel Pickering and Edith Thatcher. Mrs Pickering recognized Loughans's Yorkshire accent because her husband came from there. Edith Thatcher had lent him a pillow, and because she had left the station early in the morning, she had retrieved it from under his head while he was still sleeping. This was at 5.45 in the morning. Both women had seen the hand with no fingers.

The three women were followed by James Rycroft, a railway re-layer. That Sunday night in November he had come to do some work at the station. He knew all three women by sight and saw Loughans with them, remembering him because the man had four fingers missing on his right hand.

The next witness was William Bull, a ganger employed by the London Passenger Board, who produced records to show that James Rycroft had worked at Warren Street station, concreting and cleaning, on the night of 28/29th, and that was the only night in November he had done so.

Cross-examination could shake none of the witnesses. It looked as if Loughans had an unshakeable alibi. If he had been at Warren Street station from 11.30 at night to 5.45 in the morning he couldn't possibly have been in Portsmouth between two and four in the morning. No man can be in two places at once.

The jury were confused. They could not reconcile his detailed confession with his unshakeable alibi. After two hours' discussion they were hopelessly deadlocked. Coming back into court, the jury's foreman asked the judge's direction on a particular point. 'Had the prosecution had a reasonable time to investigate the alibi, seeing that it was brought forward at the last minute, so to speak?'

The judge pointed out that the accused was not bound to disclose his defence. And the mere fact that it had not been disclosed earlier was no grounds for rejecting it. The jury went back to continue their deliberations.

Nearly two hours later the jury filed back into court and the foreman said that they could not agree on a verdict. Prosecuting counsel breathed again as His Lordship discharged the jury and said that the case would be retried. It would be transferred to the Old Bailey as it would take too long to wait for a retrial at Winchester.

In the event it was only a fortnight later when the case went on at the Central Criminal court in London. But in the meantime, Casswell had done some homework, as he describes in his book *A Lance for Liberty*.

Reading carefully the evidence of the four witnesses who had seen Loughans at Warren Street station, he noticed that there was only one who actually claimed to have seen him between 12.30 and 5.45 in the morning. And that was Mrs Edna Costors. She got up at about three o'clock and said she'd seen him in his bunk. But if she'd just woken up she might still have been half asleep and could have made a mistake. And if she had, then Loughans didn't have an alibi for that period. What Casswell had to find out was: could Loughans have travelled from Warren Street to Portsmouth, committed the burglary and got back by 5.45 a.m.?

He got in touch with the Portsmouth police and the result was that on the night of 20/21 March 1944, Detective Constables Thyne and Luker of the Portsmouth CID, set out from Warren Street station in a twelve horsepower Riley at 11.50 p.m. They drove to Portsmouth and reached the John Barleycorn at 1.57 a.m. They stayed there until 2.30 a.m., allowing half an hour for the burglary and the murder, then set out for London again, arriving at Warren Street at 4.35 a.m. And they estimated that conditions on the road were far worse than they had been on the Sunday night of the murder.

So Loughans could have made the journey from London to Portsmouth on that fateful night and still have been back in his bunk in time to be seen by the women at 5.45 a.m.

The second trial began at the Old Bailey on Tuesday, 28 March 1944, before Mr Justice Cassells, the counsel being the same as for the first. As required by court procedure the new evidence from the prosecution was served on the accused before the trial. But Casswell had a problem: should he present his additional evidence along with the rest of the prosecution case, which in a murder trial is normally presented first, or should he wait until the defence had produced their alibi witnesses? After all he couldn't be sure that the defence would produce those witnesses and it would be foolish to produce rebuttal evidence until there was something to rebut. Casswell decided to wait until the defence had presented their case.

But once again defence counsel, John Maude KC, caught the prosecution off-guard. Casswell was astonished when he heard Maude say: 'I now call my next witness, Sir Bernard Spilsbury.'

Sir Bernard Spilsbury's name would have caused a sensation in any courtroom in the country. The most eminent pathologist of his day, his appearances in court were legendary. He featured in most of the great trials of the first half of the century, from that of Crippen in 1910 to the de Antiquis case in 1947. He seemed to have a mesmeric effect on juries and his authority in forensic pathology was almost unquestioned. This was rather unfortunate in the Loughans trial because by then Sir Bernard was nearing the end of his life. Having suffered a stroke a couple of years before and continuing to overwork, his strength was failing and his judgements were perhaps not quite as good as they had been.

Sir Bernard said that he had gone to Brixton Prison to interview Loughans. 'I asked him if he would grip my hand as in the action of shaking hands. Then I asked him if he would hold my hand with all the strength he had. His grip was weak and flabby,' concluded Spilsbury. Then he took a deep breath and made his pronouncement. 'I do not believe that he could strangle anyone with that hand.'

This evidence obviously influenced the jury, particularly as Maude in his cross-examination of Dr Simpson drew from him the admission that he had not actually examined Loughans's hand, but had based his judgement on a plaster cast and photographs.

But Casswell still had one trick up his sleeve: his

rebuttal evidence. Yet when he stood up to call the witnesses, Mr Justice Cassells said: 'No, Mr Casswell, I'll not have it!'

In vain did the prosecuting counsel protest. 'But, my Lord, the needs of justice demand that this new evidence be heard.'

'If you wanted to present this evidence, you should have done so at the first hearing.'

Casswell sat back in despair and disbelief. How could he have produced this evidence at the first trial? The alibi had been sprung upon him during the trial and he'd had no time to gather his rebuttal evidence. He knew now that he had lost the case. And so it proved. The jury took just an hour to bring in a verdict of not guilty. And Loughans walked free.

Well, not quite. There was that little matter of the old lady at St Albans whom he had tied to a bed with electric flex and robbed. As he descended the steps of the Old Bailey two police officers approached and rearrested him. And unfortunately for Loughans the evidence against him was overwhelming this time, since the old lady had no difficulty recognizing him as the man who had assaulted and robbed her. Loughans received seven years' penal servitude.

That really should have been the end of the story. But there were still more astonishing developments in this amazing tale, though they took sixteen years to come.

During that time Casswell had finally retired and written his memoirs. But the fact that he had not been allowed by Mr Justice Cassells to present his rebuttal evidence at the second trial had always rankled with him, and in *A Lance for Liberty*, he mentioned this in the chapter on the case. Although he was careful not to dispute the verdict he did suggest that if he had been allowed to give his evidence it might have had some effect on the jury.

Before the book was published extracts of it appeared in a series of articles in the *People* newspaper. The article on the Loughans case was headed, 'THIS IS THE PERFECT MURDER', and appeared in the 18 December 1960 issue.

At the time, Loughans was serving a sentence of ten years' preventive detention in Wormwood Scrubs and read the article in prison. He took exception to its content and began a libel action against the publishers of the newspaper, the editor and Mr J.D. Casswell in the High Court, in January 1963.

Mr Patrick O'Connor, QC, who appeared for Loughans told the jury that they 'were going to have to try again a murder trial in the guise of a libel action'. For one of the defences against libel is that the words used were true.

Yet the libel trial was not quite a re-run of the murder trials which had already taken place. Mr J.C. Molony QC, who appeared for the defendants, was able to question Loughans about his appalling criminal history, a procedure which would have been impossible in a criminal trial.

Another difference was that Sir Bernard Spilsbury had died in the intervening years and the plaintiff's new pathologist, Dr Francis Camps, although an able medical witness, did not have the former's God-like authority. Dr Keith Simpson, now a professor, again gave his testimony. He had examined Loughans's hand this time and gave it as his opinion that it was quite capable of strangulation, even after all these years. He was still convinced that it had been responsible for Mrs Robinson's death.

Not all the Warren Street witnesses were now available. Mrs Edna Costors had remarried and moved away and could not be traced. But the other four witnesses went into the box and repeated their testimony that Loughans had been at the station on the night of 28/29 November 1943.

But this time the rebuttal evidence was introduced and the two policemen, now both retired, came forward to describe the journey they had made by car from Warren Street to Portsmouth soon after the first trial.

It was enough to convince the jury. After a three-hour

deliberation, their reply to the question, 'Did the words of
the article mean that the plaintiff was guilty of and
committed the murder of Rose Ada Robinson?', was yes.

And to the question: 'Were the words true in substance
and in fact?' the answer was again: yes.

Three months later Harold Loughans, now with
inoperable cancer, walked into the offices of the *People* and
confessed that he had murdered Rose Robinson in
Portsmouth nearly twenty years before. The newspaper
published his confession on 26 May 1963. Loughans died
two years later in Hammersmith Hospital, still technically
serving a prison sentence.

3   Donald Merrett:
A Murderous Disguise

Mrs Henrietta Sutherland was stoking the kitchen fire when she heard the shot.

It seemed to come from the sitting-room and was immediately followed by a woman's scream and the sound of a falling body.

She jumped to her feet with alarm, wiping her hands automatically on her apron. There came the sound of heavy footfalls approaching. Mrs Sutherland, who was a young woman and not very brave, cringed back, looking for somewhere to hide. She heard the thudding of books being dropped on to the floor in the hall and nearly jumped out of her skin with fright.

The door opened suddenly and framed in the space stood a tall figure. He was a heavily built young man with a large nose which dominated his face. Relief flooded over Mrs Sutherland as she recognized the son of her employer, Mrs Merrett. But although he was big the young man was only seventeen years old; his face was crumpled and he looked as if he was going to cry.

'Rita,' he mumbled, 'Mother's shot herself!'

The maid's mind seemed to go numb. All she could say was: 'Why, Mr Donald? She seemed all right when I saw her a few minutes ago.'

The young man slumped heavily on to a kitchen chair

and covered his face with his hands. Through his fingers came a low voice. 'She said I'd been wasting her money. And she quarrelled with me about it.'

The young woman's hands fluttered like small birds. She didn't know what to do. 'Shouldn't we …? Is she …?'

Abruptly the large young man climbed to his feet. He turned and left the way he had come. The maid followed him into the hall. There on the ground was the heap of books Donald Merrett had dropped in his precipitate rush to the kitchen. He was a student at Edinburgh University and could be seen every morning leaving the house at 31 Buckingham Terrace with a pile of books under his arm. Mrs Sutherland skirted the books and followed Donald into the sitting-room.

It was nearly eighteen feet square, not particularly large for a sitting-room in 1926. Over against the far wall was a bureau and between it and the door an oval gate-legged table. On the floor, between the bureau and the table, lay Mrs Merrett.

A plump woman in her fifties, she was lying on her back. There was a great deal of blood on both the floor beside her and her head. On the top of the bureau Mrs Sutherland noticed a pistol she had never seen before. She went towards the prone figure on the floor with trepidation, frightened by all the blood, and noticed that the injured woman was still breathing.

The voice of Donald Merrett came from behind her. 'Help me get her on to the settee, Rita.'

The young woman shrank back. 'Oh, I couldn't. I couldn't touch her.'

The young man shrugged his shoulders. 'Let's leave her then. I can't stand to look at her any longer.' He led the way out of the room.

'What shall we do, Mr Donald?'

Donald Merrett stroked his chin importantly. 'We must telephone the police,' he said.

After phoning they stood waiting in the hall. Eventually

two policemen, Constables Middlemiss and Izatt, arrived with an ambulance. As Mrs Merrett was being stretchered out to the vehicle, PC Middlemiss took out his notebook and licked the end of his pencil.

'Now sir, if you could just let me know what happened to the poor lady?'

The burly Donald Merrett sat down on a chair in the room where his mother had previously been lying on the floor. 'Well, we'd just had breakfast. Mrs Sutherland had cleared the things away. And I was sitting over there reading.' He pointed to an easy chair over the other side of the room. 'My mother was at the table writing letters. I heard a shot and looked up to see her falling to the floor.' He went on to explain how he had gone into the kitchen to tell the maid and they had phoned the police.

'And why, sir, would the good lady do such a thing?' asked the constable, looking down at the young man with the big nose.

'Money matters.'

'Ah,' said the constable as if he felt that this might shed a great deal of light on things. 'Now what do you mean by "money matters"? Too much or too little?'

'Just money matters,' said Donald Merrett shortly.

While Merrett went with his mother in the ambulance the two policemen took the opportunity to look round the room. Constable Middlemiss saw the gun on top of the bureau and noted that it was bloodstained. He took a piece of paper from his pocket and carefully wrapped the pistol in it – not, however, to preserve the fingerprints, but to prevent the blood getting on his clothes. Afterwards he couldn't remember whether he had picked up the gun from the floor or the bureau. The other constable was convinced that he had seen his colleague retrieve the gun from the floor.

The two constables reported the case as one of attempted suicide.

Mrs Merrett was taken to the Edinburgh Royal

Infirmary where she was placed in Ward 3, the felons' ward, which had bars on the windows and doors with substantial locks, for in 1926 attempted suicide was a criminal offence.

When she was examined by Dr Holcombe he found that she had a bullet-wound through her right ear. He carefully washed away the blood, but did not discover the characteristic blackening or 'tattooing' which a pistol fired close to the skin usually produces. An X-ray picture showed that the small-calibre nickel-plated bullet was lodged at the base of her skull. In those days it was impossible to operate. There was nothing more that could be done.

Donald Merrett did not remain long at the hospital. Having seen his mother settled in he was soon off to the Dunedin Palais de Danse, a dance hall in Picardy Place, Edinburgh, where he met his usual dancing-partner, Betty Christie. She was a hostess who could be 'booked out' by the hour or, at fifteen shillings, for a whole afternoon. The young man reserved her for the afternoon and took her to Queensferry on his motorcycle.

In fact Donald Merrett spent most of his afternoons at the dance hall.

He had been born in New Zealand in August 1908. His father was an electrical engineer and soon afterwards the family moved to St Petersburg in Russia. But the climate there did not suit the child and Mrs Bertha Merrett, who had private means of her own, took her young son to Switzerland, leaving her husband behind in Russia. She never saw her husband again. Mrs Merrett spent the 1914–18 War in Switzerland then afterwards went back to New Zealand. In 1924, when her only child Donald was sixteen, she brought him to England to finish his education. He spent a year at Malvern College, but although his academic progress was good (he had a natural aptitude for languages), his conduct was not. After some trouble with a local girl his mother abandoned her

idea of sending him to Oxford and looked round for a
university where he could live at home and she could keep
an eye on him. She eventually decided upon Edinburgh
University and Donald enrolled there early in 1926.

But without telling his mother the young man soon
dropped out. He would leave each morning with his books
underneath his arm and return in the evening looking
suitably tired, but without having been anywhere near the
university in the meantime. After dinner he would lock
himself in his bedroom, 'so that he would not be disturbed
in his studies,' he said. Then he would take off the rope he
had strung across the window – to prevent his falling out
when he walked in his sleep, he had told his mother – and
with its help, climb down to the street and make his way to
the Palais de Danse.

While Donald Merrett was taking Betty Christie out on
his motorcycle the police paid another visit to 31
Buckingham Terrace. Inspector Fleming of the local CID
was accompanied by Sergeant Henderson. They interviewed Mrs Sutherland and made a cursory examination of
the sitting-room, noting two letters to Mrs Merrett from the
Clydesdale Bank, one of them informing her that her
account was overdrawn. This seemed to confirm Donald
Merrett's remarks that his mother had been worried about
money matters. They also found the letter that Mrs Merrett
was writing before the shot was fired. It seemed a quite
chatty letter to one of her friends, but neither detective
seemed to think that it was in any way important and they
left it on the table.

Inspector Fleming went back to the police station and
wrote a report on the case and as a consequence of this a
letter was sent, from the Chief Constable of the Edinburgh
police to the Superintendent of the Royal Infirmary,
instructing him that Mrs Merrett was a prisoner charged
with attempted suicide and requesting that the police be
notified of the date of her discharge so that she might be
taken into custody.

Because of this, when Mrs Merrett recovered consciousness she was not told what had happened to her.

She seemed quite lucid as she asked the nursing sister: 'Why am I here?'

'You've had a little accident,' replied Sister Grant, soothingly.

'What sort of accident?' The middle-aged lady with her head swathed in bandages was obviously in a great deal of pain.

'Can't you tell me?' enquired the nurse.

Mrs Merrett frowned in concentration. 'I seem to remember writing a letter. Then a bang went off in my head like a pistol.'

'Was there a pistol there?' asked Sister Grant, cautiously.

'I don't know. Was there?'

The nurse decided to change the subject. 'Are you sure you were writing when ... when this occurred?'

'Of course I'm sure. You can ask Donald if you like. He was standing beside me waiting for me to finish the letter so he could post it on his way to the university.'

This conversation was also heard by Nurse Innes and together the two nurses reported it to Dr Holcombe.

The next day he in turn asked Mrs Merrett how the accident had happened.

'I was sitting at my table writing letters and Donald was standing beside me. "Go away, Donald," I said, "you're annoying me." The next thing was that there was a bang in my head and I don't remember anything more.'

Even though the second story was slightly different to the first, Dr Holcombe thought it sufficiently important to report it to the police. Inspector Fleming called at the hospital and was told by Dr Holcombe that although Mrs Merrett was fully conscious she was gravely ill and the chances of her recovering were slight. But although the inspector listened to the statements of the doctor and the nurses he failed to take one from Mrs Merrett.

Mrs Merrett's sister, Mrs Penn, who was holidaying in the South of France with her husband, was informed of the tragedy and the Penns arrived in Edinburgh on the morning of 24 March, just a week after the shooting. They found Mrs Merrett conscious and pleased to see them. She repeated what she had told other people, but added something rather significant. She said she was sitting at the writing table when an explosion went off in her head – 'as if Donald had shot me'.

Mrs Penn replied that such a thing was impossible and the subject was dropped.

Mrs Merrett asked the Penns to move into the apartment in Buckingham Terrace and look after Donald. During her stay there the question of what had happened to her sister occupied Mrs Penn's mind a great deal. One night she asked Donald outright if he had shot his mother. The young man replied hotly that he had not, arguing that it was attempted suicide. This was equally abhorrent to Mrs Penn, who claimed that her sister would never have taken her own life, and eventually they settled for Mrs Merrett's having shot herself accidentally.

A few days later Mr Penn was sitting in the room in which Mrs Merrett had been shot when he noticed something on the floor. It was an empty cartridge case, presumably from the round which had been fired at Mrs Merrett. He communicated with the police and Inspector Fleming called to see them. At this stage, nearly a fortnight after the shooting, he finally decided to take a formal statement from Donald Merrett.

'Can you tell me when you first bought the pistol?'

Merrett sat thinking for some time. 'I think it was some time in February.'

'And for what purpose did you buy the gun?'

'Well,' said the young man, 'we were thinking of going abroad for the Easter holidays, and I wanted to shoot rabbits.'

Experts afterwards gave it as their opinion that the

pistol, of Spanish origin with a 0.25 calibre, was totally unsuitable for the stated purpose.

'And did your mother approve of your purchase?' asked the inspector suavely.

'Er ... well, no. She took the gun away from me and put it in her desk. I told her to be careful with it as it was loaded. But I never saw the gun again until the day she shot herself.'

Further questioning elicited the fact that he had picked up the pistol from the floor after his mother had shot herself and placed it on the bureau.

The inspector decided to change direction. 'Will you let me have the letter your mother was writing when she was shot?'

The heavily built young man looked uncomfortable. 'Unfortunately, I cannot. I destroyed it, you see, because it had her blood on it.'

The inspector didn't remember the letter's having blood on it, but he said nothing more on that subject.

He also questioned Donald about his mother's finances and took away with him her bank-book, cheque-book and the letter the bank had sent her about being overdrawn.

Mrs Bertha Merrett died in Edinburgh Royal Infirmary on 1 April, a fortnight after she had been admitted. The cause of death was reported as basal meningitis, following a bullet wound in the cranium. The post-mortem was conducted by Professor Harvey Littlejohn of Edinburgh University. He reported that:

> The direction of the wound, judging by the external wounds and the position of the bullet, was horizontal and slightly from behind ... the bullet lying about an inch anterior to the external wound ... There was nothing to indicate the distance at which the discharge of the weapon took place, whether from a few inches or a greater distance. So far as the position of the wound is concerned, the case is consistent with suicide.

After his mother's death Donald continued to live with his aunt and uncle and to frequent the Dunedin Palais de Danse. Under the terms of Mrs Merrett's will the public trustee had the handling of Donald Merrett's affairs. Because of his continual absences the University of Edinburgh refused to allow him to return and it was thought best to put him under the care of a private tutor, with a view to preparing him to go to Oxford. He was therefore sent to the vicarage of Hughenden, near High Wycombe, to continue his studies.

When the public trustee began an examination of Mrs Merrett's financial affairs he found that she had an account with the Midland Bank. When she moved to Edinburgh she opened an account with the Clydesdale Bank, which was kept in funds by the cheques drawn upon the Midland account. But between 2 February and 17 March, the day that she was shot, a number of cheques had been cashed by her son at the Clydesdale Bank. They had been made out to him and signed Bertha Merrett. As a result, the account went rapidly into the red. In fact a letter was sent to Mrs Merrett on 13 March pointing out that the account was in danger of becoming overdrawn and suggesting that she transfer funds from the Midland Bank. And then on 16 March a letter was sent saying that her account was now overdrawn.

It was noticed too that the cheques cashed by Donald Merrett were not in sequence with other cheques, but were taken mostly from the back of the cheque book. The counterfoils had also been removed. When the cheques were examined by experts it became quite clear that Mrs Merrett's signature had been forged, mainly by being traced on to the cheques using carbon paper, and then inked over afterwards.

The reason for the deception was not hard to discover. The young man received ten shillings a week pocket-money from his mother, and it cost him more than that to book Betty Christie for one afternoon, to say nothing of the rings he had bought her and the second-hand motor-cycle he had bought himself.

When the police finally came to consider this evidence it became quite obvious that the suicide theory was not foolproof. The opinions of friends and neighbours were that Mrs Merrett was an extremely level-headed woman and would be very unlikely to kill herself in the middle of writing a letter. Another explanation was that the two letters from the bank would eventually have alerted Mrs Merrett to what her son was doing, and to avoid this he had shot her.

In view of these suspicions Professor Littlejohn began to have second thoughts about the conclusions he had drawn from his autopsy. He embarked on a series of experiments, firing Merrett's gun, from various distances, at moistened white paper. In all cases, where the distance of the gun from the paper was consistent with suicide, he found blackening on the paper. Some of it could be washed off, but there was still an easily discernible residue always left. And he recalled that Dr Holcombe had found no such residue on Mrs Merrett's skin. These experiments were extended, with the help of John Glaister, Professor of Forensic Medicine at the University of Glasgow, to fresh human skin taken from an amputated leg. The results were the same.

Donald Merrett was arrested at Hughenden in December 1926, nine months after the shooting occurred. The trial began on 1 February 1927, before the Lord Justice-Clerk, Lord Alness. The prosecution was in the hands of the Lord Advocate, the Right Hon. William Watson, KC, and the defence was led by Mr Craigie Aitchison, KC.

There were two charges, one of murder and the other of uttering forged cheques.

From the very beginning, it was obvious that the prosecution did not have a strong case. Because Inspector Fleming and his constables had not bothered to fingerprint the gun, secure the letter Mrs Merrett was writing when she was shot or take a statement from the lady while she was still alive, there was little direct evidence linking Donald Merrett with the shooting.

The prosecution therefore had to rely on the evidence of Professor Littlejohn, Professor Glaister and Dr Holcombe. But doubt was cast, by defence counsel, on Professor Littlejohn's evidence because he had changed his mind, at first saying suicide was possible, then saying it was not. And Dr Holcombe was accused of not using a hand lens to search for blackening on Mrs Merrett's skin.

Then Mr Aitchison brought on his big guns. Sir Bernard Spilsbury had come up from London to give evidence for the defence. He too had conducted experiments, similar to those of Professor Littlejohn, with the assistance of Robert Churchill, a London gunsmith whose reputation as a firearms expert was almost as illustrious as Spilsbury's as a pathologist. Their results directly contradicted Littlejohn's, although no one seemed to notice that they didn't even use the same gun as the one which had shot Mrs Merrett. Nevertheless Spilsbury's opinion – that neither the site nor the direction of the bullet was inconsistent with suicide, and that the bleeding and rubbing of the wound might well have removed the blackening – obviously influenced the jury.

The jury numbered fifteen, six women and nine men. After an hour's deliberation they brought in a verdict of not proven on the murder charge, by a majority, and on the charge of uttering forged cheques, a unanimous verdict of guilty. It was afterwards learned that the majority for the first charge was five for guilty and ten for not proven. 'Not proven' is a curious verdict, used in Scotland and some other countries, which without giving the connotation of innocence, nevertheless allows the prisoner to go free. Merrett, however, was sentenced to twelve months' imprisonment on the charge of uttering.

He was visited in prison by, among other people, one of

his mother's friends, Mrs Mary Bonnar, who brought him small gifts and strongly believed in his innocence. While Merrett was still in prison she married again, to a Sir William Menzies, and thereafter always called herself Lady Menzies. But she was a staunch Roman Catholic and although she agreed to a Protestant wedding, when later her husband refused to embrace the Catholic faith she left him and his castle in Scotland, and went to live in Hastings.

When Donald Merrett was released from prison in October 1927 he was invited by Lady Menzies to come and stay with her and her daughter Vera in Hastings. The seventeen-year-old Vera and Donald, who was just nineteen, got on very well together – so well that the following May they eloped to Scotland and were married at Govan Registry Office.

Vera, who was a devout Roman Catholic like her mother, afterwards insisted on a Roman Catholic wedding. Merrett agreed and himself became a Catholic, a faith which was to remain with him all his life.

He bought a second-hand car, a tent and some provisions, and they set off on a camping honeymoon. But they soon ran out of money and Merrett began writing cheques which had no funds to back them. The shopkeepers complained to the police and the couple was arrested just outside Newcastle upon Tyne.

Donald Merrett, who was now calling himself Ronald John Chesney, was sentenced to six months. There was no evidence that Vera had ordered any goods and she was released and went back to Hastings.

Chesney was let out in January 1929 and he went to live in the flat Vera had found them in Hastings. Lady Menzies soon moved in with them. In August of that year, when he was twenty-one, Chesney came into the fortune left him by his maternal grandfather – some £50,000 – and since he also had the income from the money his mother had left him, he was a comparatively rich man.

Later that year he went to see the public trustee, who had the handling of the fortune, and was persuaded to make a marriage settlement of £8,500 on Vera. She was to have the interest on the money for her lifetime but if she died before him the money would revert to him.

Chesney began to live the life of a country squire. He bought several sports-cars and a twenty-room mansion in Weybridge. But he soon tired of this and, through men he had met in prison, joined a smuggling gang based in the East End of London. Eventually he purchased a two-seater aeroplane which he used for smuggling trips to the Continent. Soon after that he sold up the house in Weybridge and bought a pilot cutter.

By this time Chesney had grown to look the part. Always a tall and heavily built man he now sported a black beard and an earring in his left ear. With his yachting cap set at a rakish angle he looked like a pirate as he set sail with his wife, two children and the ever-present Lady Menzies for a tour of the Mediterranean.

He spent the pre-war years on smuggling trips round the Mediterranean, but in 1939, with the threat of war looming, he sent his family back to England by train, while he flew his plane back from France. When he arrived he found that Vera and her mother had bought a large house in Ealing which they were going to convert into a guest-home for old people. But Chesney, who could not stay in any one place for long, went off to join the Navy.

It seems incredible that in spite of his prison record he was immediately commissioned. And by 1941 he was back in the Mediterranean, commanding a schooner. The vessel was sunk, however, and he was captured, then repatriated, and went on to spend most of the rest of the war at Scapa Flow.

A few days after war ended, he was sent to Germany, because of his knowledge of the language. Stationed just outside Hamburg, Chesney was in his element. He was now a Lieutenant-Commander and had the use of several cars and a Jeep.

There were unrivalled opportunities for operating on the black market. The German population, short of commodities like food, soap and cigarettes, was prepared to barter family heirlooms and antiques, jewellery, cameras, watches and even furniture and carpets for them. It was a golden opportunity for men in the occupying forces, like Chesney, to make money.

He acquired a German girlfriend, the beautiful dark-haired Gerda Schaller, and embarked upon a riotous life of fast cars, drinking, gambling and dealing on the black market. When he was finally demobilized he joined the Control Commission in Germany and continued as before. But almost everything Chesney attempted was done to excess. He stole a luxurious Porsche, which had once belonged to Admiral Dönitz, and had a wild week in Paris with Gerda before he was finally arrested. Convicted by a court martial, he was sentenced to four months' imprisonment, which he served in England.

But instead of returning to Vera he went back to Gerda. He asked Vera for a divorce, but being a good Catholic she refused and continued to demand maintenance from him.

He was now travelling on his smuggling assignments with Gerda, who was a refugee from the Russian zone in Germany and had no proper papers. Chesney gave her a forged passport, but they were arrested in France and the forgery was discovered. Gerda was sentenced to six months for using the passport and Chesney to four for supplying it.

Things were now getting too hot for him in Europe and, without waiting for Gerda to be released, he went back to England and Vera, after serving his sentence. But she was now beginning to drink heavily. Rows between them increased and Chesney found that he was missing Gerda. He returned to Germany.

But Gerda had had enough of the uncertain life with Chesney and they parted. He soon found himself another girlfriend, however, a pretty blonde German hostess in a nightclub. Her name was Sonia Winnicke. She was twenty-four and lived with her parents, who had a grocer's shop outside Cologne. Although by this time Chesney was forty-two she became the new love of his life. He went back to England to plead with Vera for a divorce, but again she refused. While he was in England he attempted to smuggle coffee and English currency out of the country, but he was arrested by customs officials at Newhaven and sentenced to twelve months' imprisonment.

It was while he was in Wandsworth prison that he began to think about another murder. If Vera could be got rid of he would be free to marry Sonia and would also be better off to the tune of some £10,000 – since the £8,500 he had settled on her all those years ago would be worth about that by now and it would come to him on her death.

But he couldn't interest the hardened criminals with whom he discussed the project in prison. They even refused the £1,000 he was offering anyone who would knock Vera down with a motor car one foggy morning.

When Chesney was released he lived for a while with Sonia in Earl's Court. One evening when they were drinking together in a local pub a friend came up to them. 'Here Ches, there's someone I want you to meet.'

He turned to indicate a bulky, middle-aged man whose face was vaguely familiar. Chesney stood up politely and shook the stranger's hand, but there was a questioning look on his face as he glanced at his friend.

'Don't you see?' his friend laughed. 'Look, stand together, you two. Now, what do you think, Sonia? Don't you think they look alike?'

Sonia studied the two men standing side by side. 'I suppose so,' she said doubtfully. 'If Ches shaved off his beard and wore glasses he might look like him.'

It was a small incident, but it remained in Chesney's mind. He afterwards found that the man's name was

Leslie Chown, a photographer. A plot was beginning to hatch in Chesney's fertile brain. A little while after this he shaved off his beard.

'I'm going to remain clean-shaven,' he announced, 'until Vera gives me a divorce.'

Next he went to Somerset House and obtained a copy of Chown's birth certificate; then to the nearest post office to get a passport application form. He bought himself a pair of horn-rimmed spectacles like Chown's, removed the earring, smoothed his hair down and had himself photographed. The result looked remarkably like Chown.

It was then a simple matter to forge the signature of a doctor he knew, and send off the photograph and copy of the birth certificate to obtain a passport in Chown's name. That gave Chesney an alias. The next thing he decided upon was a dummy run.

He and Sonia went back to Cologne. For some time he stayed with Sonia and her parents, serving in the grocer's shop and letting his beard and moustache grow.

On 2 February 1954, leaving Sonia behind, he took a train from Cologne to the Hook of Holland and crossed on the ferry to Harwich. From there he went to London and booked into a hotel in Earls Court. On the train journey, he took pains to advertise his presence, making a special point of asking the ticket inspectors questions, so that they would remember him.

The next day he called at the old people's home in Montpelier Road, Ealing. Vera was surprised to see him, but he had brought a bottle of gin to help smooth relations between them. He explained that he'd come over to do some business in London. Later that night he took her to the pictures, making sure that the girl in the ticket-office remembered him, then he returned Vera to Montpelier Road and her mother. He said good-night to both of them, then returned to Earls Court.

He booked out of his hotel the next morning and returned to Cologne on 4 February, well satisfied with the way things had gone. People would remember that he had gone to see his wife Vera, but they would also remember that she was alive after he had left.

Two days later, on Saturday, 6 February, he took Sonia with him to Amsterdam where they booked into the Frifo Hotel. She had no knowledge of his plans, thinking that it was to be a weekend spent shopping and seeing the sights of the city. On Tuesday morning he put her on a train for Cologne, saying that he had some business to attend to and would join her shortly at her parents' home. Then he went back to the hotel and shaved off his beard and moustache. Smoothing down his hair he put on the horn-rimmed spectacles and became Mr Chown. He took a taxi to Amsterdam airport.

But there he hit his first snag. Thick fog at the airport meant that all flights had been cancelled. He hung around waiting for the fog to lift, but it persisted all day and well into the next. The earliest flight he could get was at 6.30 on Wednesday evening.

When he landed in England he phoned Vera from the airport, telling her that he was engaged in a secret deal and could she put him up for the night? Knowing Chesney, Vera guessed that the secret deal was probably illegal, a situation to which she was well accustomed. He made her promise not to tell anybody he was coming and particularly not to let anybody know that he had been with her. And he promised her a substantial cut of the profits if the deal went off satisfactorily.

It was getting on for midnight when he arrived in Ealing, and when Vera saw the two bottles of gin he had brought she was more than pleased to see him. Questioned about his disguise, Chesney said it was connected with his secret deal and Vera accepted this. They were both undressed, ready for bed, by the time they were well down the first bottle. Vera had already had a few by the time Chesney arrived and it wasn't long before she was flat-out in her chair.

He walked along to the nearby bathroom and half filled the tub. Then, leaving the bathroom door open, he went back to Vera's room.

'Come on my beauty,' he said, lifting the unresisting woman on to his shoulder. He carried her to the bathroom.

It took only a few minutes to dump Vera into the bath and hold her head under the water until she drowned. When she was found, the level of alcohol in her blood would indicate that she had fallen in to the bath in a drunken stupor and drowned.

He carefully wiped off his fingerprints from the bottles and anything else he had touched, got dressed again and crept downstairs. At the bottom of the stairs he listened. There were still a few people moving about on the second floor, but nobody knew that he was here.

It was the perfect murder. Not like that clumsy affair twenty-seven years ago when he'd been so lucky to get away with shooting his mother. All he had to do now was to cross the hall quietly, open the front door and nobody would know that he had ever been there.

He listened for the last time, then stepped forward.

Lady Menzies came out of one of the ground-floor bedrooms carrying a tray with a coffee-pot on it.

'Oh hello, Donald. What are you doing here at this time of night?'

Chesney grabbed the antique pewter coffee-pot and swung it at her head. Lady Menzies went down on her knees. But the old lady fought back like a wildcat. She bit and she scratched, and was only subdued when Chesney managed to get a stocking round her neck and hold it tight. He dumped her body under a pile of cushions in a back room.

But he knew that it had all gone wrong. As he made his way back to Germany he realized that he was carrying the signs of a fierce fight, and that when the bodies were discovered the next morning there would be an intensive police investigation and he would be the number-one suspect.

But he must have been surprised at how quickly the papers got on to him. Within a few days they carried the story that the police were looking for him. He was identified as the man who had once been accused of murdering his mother; one newspaper even published interviews with some of the ex-prisoners with whom Chesney had served at Wandsworth, and who claimed that he had offered them money to murder his wife.

Initially, his plan was to run for it. South America perhaps. And he would take Sonia with him. But she refused to see him. When he phoned he was told that she was not there. When he went to the shop he was told she had gone away for a few days. He turned away in despair.

He was found the next day in a wood just outside Cologne, shot through the head. Letters in his pocket indicated that he had left everything he owned to Sonia.

The police were later able to establish that the scratches on Chesney's arms and hands had been caused by Lady Menzies' fingernails. Bloodstains on his trousers were shown to be of her blood group. The jury at the inquest into the deaths of Vera and Lady Menzies had no difficulty in coming to the conclusion that he had committed both murders.

There was only one mourner at Chesney's funeral in Cologne: the beautiful dark-haired Gerda Schaller, who had shared his life for seven years. Afterwards, she told a reporter that, years before, Chesney had boasted to her that he had shot his mother. But she hadn't believed him. He was always such a liar.

4 Harry Thaw:
Show-girl Show-down

'Why, there's nobody here,' said the young girl looking round the room. 'Where's the other people?'

She was only sixteen years old, but already had an ethereal beauty much in demand from photographers and the public alike. Her thick black hair hung down below her shoulders and shone in the artificial light, and her large blue eyes, which in the future would cause many a heart to flutter, looked up at the man by her side.

He was a complete contrast. Tall and heavily built, he was in his fifties with startling red hair and a bristling moustache of the same colour, which made him look more like a wild Corsair than the brilliant New York architect he was. He looked down at the young girl and smiled.

'What do you think? They must have turned us down.'

'Oh, that's too bad.' She pouted prettily. 'Then we won't be able to have a party.' She looked round the sumptuously decorated room and noted that the dining-table was laid for only two people.

'Not only have they turned us down but they've probably gone off somewhere and forgotten all about us,' said the big man with the red hair.

'Had I better go home then?' asked the young girl shyly.

For this was America in 1901, and she knew as well as anyone that it was unthinkable for a young female to remain in the presence of a male who was not a close relative, without a chaperon. On the other hand, this was New York, the centre of 'advanced thinking' and behaviour in America at the time. And though she lived with her mother she was in the chorus of the hit musical *Florodora* – from which comes the famous lines: 'Tell me pretty maiden / Are there any more at home like you?' – and could be said to be on the fringes of Bohemian society.

The man, Stanford White, was probably the most famous architect in New York at the time. Rich and successful, he was still an active member of café and Bohemian society, although he had a wife and a son at Harvard.

'No, my dear,' he said. 'You must be tired after your evening at the theatre. Take off your hat and coat and sit down. We'll have some food just to spite all those who haven't come.'

The young girl made a show of reluctance, but she sat down opposite the red-headed man. Her face had a teasing look as she said, 'And will you restrict me to my usual one glass of champagne?'

'Certainly,' said White, pouring her a generous glass of the wine. 'I've promised your mother to look after you while she's away in Pittsburgh, and I won't let her down.'

'You gave her money to go on the trip, didn't you?'

'Now Evelyn.' The big man waggled an admonishing finger at the girl across the table. 'There's absolutely no harm in a chap like me, who has some money to spare, helping out people who are not so well-off. Your mother's had a very difficult time bringing up you and your brother since your father died.'

'You help out quite a lot of people, don't you?' asked Evelyn Nesbit artlessly. 'A lot of the girls in the chorus of *Floradora*?'

'I do what I can, my dear,' said White holding up his glass and looking at the bubbles in it. 'I've always thought that it was important for people to have good teeth. And so I've paid for nearly all the girls at *Flora* to go to the dentist. Come on,' he said replacing the glass on the table, 'eat your food and then we'll have our own little party.'

After the meal the big man remarked: 'You've not seen all over the house have you?'

The young girl's eyes began to shine. 'Are you going to push me on your swing?'

White laughed. 'If you want me to,' he said and led her upstairs.

The house, from the outside, looked anything but opulent. It was a run-down but tall building on West 24th Street. Inside, however, all the rooms were lavishly furnished, and the upstairs room to which White took young Evelyn Nesbit contained a swing covered in red velvet. And above it, suspended near the ceiling, was a large Japanese umbrella.

'See if you can touch it,' called the big man as he pushed the young girl on the swing. Her long hair flew back and her short skirt, which came to the tops of her calf-length boots, billowed out, as she swung her legs up to try and reach the umbrella.

Evelyn's face was flushed and excited when finally she alighted from the swing. 'Come,' Stanford White took her by the hand. 'I'll show you some of the other rooms.'

He gave her a guided tour, and eventually she found herself in an extensively decorated bedroom with mirrors and pictures on the walls. Near the large double-bed was a tiny table, with a chair beside it, and on the table a small bottle of champagne and one glass.

White invited the girl to sit and began to point out to her the pictures, explaining each one as he passed round the room. Almost without her noticing, he filled the glass to the brim with wine.

He carried on talking about the pictures, then said, 'Come, Evelyn, you haven't touched your wine. Drink it up and then I'll take you home.'

The girl did as she was told and stood up. But she

experienced a peculiar sensation in her head and her legs.

'Oh dear! My legs have gone funny. And my head is spinning.'

'You've obviously drunk your champagne too quickly,' said White solicitously. 'Lie down on the bed for a while until your head clears. I'll loosen your clothes a little.'

Sometime later, Evelyn found herself in bed with no clothes on at all. Lying beside her, also without his clothes, was Stanford White. Evelyn turned her face into the pillow and began sobbing.

The big man put his hand gently on her bare shoulder. 'There, there, my dear, it's all over now.'

But Evelyn shook off his hand and carried on weeping into the pillow. Eventually White got up, put on a kimono and left the room.

Soon after she became his mistress, White set up Evelyn Nesbit and her family in a comfortable suite, with private bath, in the Hotel Audubon, just opposite the theatre where Evelyn was working. She was known as his protégée and dined with White at Delmonico's and other fashionable New York restaurants, always with other people, and went with him to parties in another of his apartments, in the Madison Square Garden Tower.

Madison Square Garden had been designed by Stanford White himself. It was used for public events like boxing bouts and horse shows, and had a roof-garden theatre as well as a ground-level arcade of shops. But its most spectacular feature was a wide 300-foot tower containing mostly private apartments.

It was there that the beautiful Evelyn Nesbit met the fashionable people from the New York theatre world. She soon found out that Stanford White had a taste for show-girls and she embarked in turn upon a number of affairs with other men. She was cited as the co-respondent in a divorce brought by the wife of one of the best-known producers in New York, and was involved with the youthful John Barrymore, later to become a star of the silent screen.

It was quite common for Evelyn, as it was for many other chorus girls, to receive flowers from wealthy young men who had seen the show. But one day in December 1901, only a few weeks after she had become White's mistress, a spray of American-beauty roses, with fifty dollar bills wrapped round the stems, was delivered to her.

This was a mere symbolic gesture, for the man who had sent the flowers, the playboy Harry Kendall Thaw, was reputed to be worth in excess of $40 million. The eldest son of the late William Thaw, a railway entrepreneur from Pittsburgh, at thirty-four he had a reputation in New York which rivalled that of Stanford White. Known as 'Mad Harry', he had already given a party for a hundred actresses, ridden his horse up the steps of his Fifth Avenue club and fought with policemen on numerous occasions. He was dedicated to the proposition that money could buy anything, including freedom from prosecution.

At first Evelyn was unimpressed with Harry Thaw, but he continued to press his intentions with gifts of money, jewellery and furs, and gradually Evelyn began to consider him in a new light.

Though under pressure from her mother to acquire the respectability of marriage, she realized that White was not available. Of the other possible suitors Thaw was easily the most affluent. The problem lay with Thaw's formidable mother, Mrs William Thaw, who had already married off one of her daughters to the Earl of Yarmouth and the other to the nephew of the fabulously wealthy Andrew Carnegie, and who didn't look kindly upon an impoverished show-girl of low birth. Harry Thaw himself was a confirmed bachelor, but he was more malleable than his mother.

Late in 1902, when Evelyn was nearly eighteen, White,

who was still her benefactor, paid for her to attend the residential acting school run by Agnes DeMille in New Jersey. It appears that this was a device connived at by both White and Evelyn's mother to get Evelyn away from New York and the attentions of the young, and at that time impecunious, John Barrymore.

While she was there she was visited by Harry Thaw, who paid for an operation she had – said to be an appendectomy. He suggested a recuperative trip to Europe for her and her mother for which, of course, he would pay. White was furious, but Evelyn was not on good terms with him because of his attempts to break up her relationship with Barrymore, and she and her mother embarked for Europe in June 1903. Thaw followed a week later.

He had rented an expensive apartment for Evelyn and her mother in Paris and it was in that city one night when they were alone that she told him of her seduction by Stanford White.

The effect on Thaw was dramatic. They had been sitting opposite each other, and when she finished her story he leapt to his feet.

'Oh, my God! Oh my God!' he sobbed, with his face in his hands. Then he began to pace the room. 'How could he do such a thing to a young child?'

Evelyn was aware that the two men had been rivals, not to say enemies, for some years, but she was surprised and frightened by the effect of her words on Thaw and she tried to defuse the situation. But he was in the grip of some powerful emotion and would not let go. He kept forcing her to tell the story over and over again until she was heartily sick of it. Eventually he calmed down and stopped talking about it, but he remained very bitter towards White.

After a holiday in Boulogne, Thaw took Evelyn and her mother to London. They stayed at Claridge's while he stayed at the Carlton Hotel. But quarrels soon broke out between Mrs Nesbit and her daughter and Thaw. She was upset at the way the young couple would go off on their own and eventually, feeling that she was no longer any use as a chaperon, returned to New York.

This was just what Evelyn and Thaw wanted. For five or six weeks, travelling as man and wife, they toured Europe. Then Thaw rented a castle in the Austrian Tyrol.

One morning he banged impatiently on Evelyn's bedroom door. 'Come on, Evelyn, breakfast's ready and the coffee's getting cold.'

She hastily put on a robe over her nightgown and came down to breakfast.

After the meal Thaw said: 'We'll go back to your room. I want to show you something you can see from your window.'

But once inside her room he closed the door behind him and, throwing her on to the bed, proceeded to thrash her with a cowhide whip hidden in his dressing-gown pocket.

In vain she screamed and pleaded for mercy. On his face was an expression of excitement and his eyes were wild and glaring. He clasped his fingers over her mouth to stifle her screams. The next morning he repeated the treatment.

Evelyn returned to New York without Thaw and managed to obtain a part in a new musical play: *The Girl from Dixie*. She was now reconciled with Stanford White, told him of Thaw's treatment of her and showed him letters Thaw had written to her, just as before she had shown Thaw letters from White. The architect was angry and persuaded Evelyn, somewhat against her will, to swear an affidavit against Thaw, describing the treatment she had had from him.

Harry Thaw returned to New York and again began pursuing Evelyn. Once more she altered her allegiances, possibly because this time Thaw was offering marriage. The wedding took place near the Thaw family home in Pittsburgh on 4 April 1904. Evelyn's mother was there

together with Mrs William Thaw, who had been persuaded
reluctantly to accept Evelyn Nesbit as a daughter-in-law
provided that her past was never mentioned.

After the wedding Harry Thaw began brooding again
about Stanford White. He tried to persuade Evelyn to sign
papers charging White with the drugging and seduction of
her as a minor, but she refused to do so. He became
obsessed with the idea that White had paid a notorious
New York gangster to have him killed and when in the city
he always carried a loaded revolver.

On 25 June of the following year Harry Thaw and his wife
were in New York, having seen his mother off on a trip to
England to visit her daughter, the Countess of Yarmouth.
In the evening Harry dined with his wife and two friends at
the Café Martin, a fashionable New York restaurant. Just
after they arrived Stanford White passed through the
dining-room on his way out with his son and a friend from
Harvard. Only Evelyn saw them leave. She asked for a
pencil then wrote a note which she passed to her husband.

The note read: 'The B— was here a minute ago, but went
out again.'

She explained later that 'B—' meant 'blackguard', a term
she and her husband regularly used for White.

After dinner they went on to the opening of a new
musical in the open-air roof theatre in Madison Square
Garden, at which the patrons sat at tables. It was nearly
eleven o'clock when the show began and a line of chorus
girls appeared on the stage. But soon after this the group
from Thaw's table got up and moved towards the back of
the room and the lifts. Evelyn Thaw led, followed by the
two friends, while the figure of Harry Thaw brought up the
rear.

Evelyn and the two men with her passed White sitting
alone at a table without giving him a second glance. But
Thaw stopped. He fumbled in his pocket. Brought out the
revolver. Levelled it at White's head and fired three times.

One bullet went through White's left eye into his brain.

Another smashed through his upper lip and lodged in the back of the skull. The other ploughed into the left shoulder. His arm, which had been resting on the table, slowly slid off as his body toppled sideways, bringing the table over as it crashed to the floor.

Thaw held the gun by the muzzle and lifted it above his head to show there was to be no more shooting, then turned and walked slowly towards the rear of the room.

Pandemonium broke out. The chorus had stopped singing and the band playing when the first shots crashed out. Many people had dived for cover. Now a hubbub of conversation arose as people looked round trying to find out what had happened.

Evelyn had rushed to rejoin her husband on hearing the shots, and seeing him with the smoking gun held high above his head called out: 'Good God, Harry! What have you done?'

'It's all right, dearie,' said Thaw calmly. 'I've probably saved your life.'

In the lobby by the lifts he was disarmed by an on-duty fireman and afterwards arrested. He offered no resistance.

'I'm glad I killed him,' he arrogantly told the constable. 'He ruined my wife.' He fumbled in his pocket. 'Here's a bill. Get Carnegie on the telephone and tell him I'm in trouble.'

Mrs William Thaw heard the news of her son's arrest when her ship docked in Liverpool; she caught the next returning liner.

'My son is innocent,' she told reporters when she landed in New York, 'and I will mobilize the entire fortune of my family to prove it.'

And she attempted to do just that. A press agent was engaged to conduct a campaign against White in the newspapers and to present Thaw as a chivalrous husband seeking to avenge the dishonouring of his wife. A play was hurriedly concocted and put on Broadway, at vast expense, depicting a character called Stanford Black as a

villainous despoiler of young virgins who was finally shot
by the virtuous Harold Daw during a performance at a
roof garden theatre.

Teams of lawyers were engaged and then dispensed
with. The first advocated pleading insanity. This was
rejected by Thaw out of hand. Another batch suggested
pleading that Thaw was temporarily insane at the time of
the shooting, but that he was now sane. This would mean,
if successful, that he would walk free. But this still did not
satisfy Thaw, who wanted a trial at which White's
debaucheries would be exposed.

A compromise was suggested by a very eminent
Californian lawyer named Delphin Delmas. He suggested
a combination of temporary insanity and the 'Unwritten
Law' in which a man was entitled to kill, given sufficient
provocation. There was no such tenet in American law,
but in the past juries had been known to acquit prisoners
along these lines.

When the trial opened on Wednesday, 23 January 1907,
it was widely regarded (and indeed remains so to this day)
as one of the most sensational trials ever staged in New
York. The courtroom was presided over by Judge
Fitzgerald, and the prosecution was in the hands of the
District Attorney, William Jerome, a cousin of Sir Winston
Churchill, who let it be known that he opposed the idea of
the Thaw millions being used to buy freedom for the son.

The defence was in the hands of a team of lawyers,
including Delphin Delmas, but led by John Gleason.
Officially, the defence was insanity – in other words they
sought a verdict of guilty but insane.

The prosecution opened by stating that the killing of
Stanford White had been a premeditated murder actuated
by jealousy. Counsel took only a couple of hours to prove,
by calling eyewitnesses, that Thaw had shot and killed
Stanford White. The defence did not cross-examine.

They opened their case with a long rambling speech by
John Gleason; he was not a courtroom lawyer and had

never before pleaded a criminal case. Everyone who heard him was left unsure as to whether Thaw's insanity was supposed to be temporary or acquired in childhood.

Gleason followed this up by calling a number of doctors to establish the insanity plea. In cross-examination, however, the district attorney tore most of their testimony to shreds, establishing that one had little knowledge of the laws of the state of New York on insanity and tripping up others on a number of technical questions.

At this stage the defence case was in tatters and Delmas declared that he would withdraw from the case unless he was put in charge. Gleason reluctantly agreed and Delmas stood up.

Immediately a change came over the courtroom. A sense of suppressed excitement affected all the participants as the short stocky figure with the leonine head and the beautiful deep voice, which had swayed so many juries in the past, began to call his witnesses.

His cleverest move, however, was to call Evelyn herself to the stand. She entered wearing a navy-blue suit, a white shirtwaist with an Eton collar and a black bow. Although twenty-two years of age she looked like a schoolgirl as she stepped into the witness-box and directed her large dark eyes at the jury. Her glance was at once demure and appealing, guaranteed to melt the heart of every member of the all-male jury.

Delmas took her through the evening of the shooting and what had happened after Thaw shot Stanford White. He then switched to her marriage, asking her for details of the wedding and who was present. Then, almost without anyone noticing, he slipped in the first of the key questions.

'When did Mr Thaw propose for the first time?'

Evelyn said that Thaw had first proposed in Paris, but that she had refused him.

'Will you tell us why you refused him?'

There was a silence and the young girl looked distressed.

'Did you tell him the reasons why you refused him?'

There was again a silence. Then came a low: 'Yes.'

'Were those reasons,' persisted the soft deep voice of
the defence counsel, 'based on any event in your life?'

Jerome jumped to his feet and objected. He could see
what was coming. What had happened in Evelyn's past
life with White was not admissible as evidence. But if she
had told her husband what had happened to her then it
was admissible, because it could be said to have had an
effect on his mind. This was Delmas's masterstroke, since
her testimony could not be subject to refutation. Whatever
she had told Thaw didn't have to be true, for present
purposes. All the jury would have to decide was whether
they believed she actually told him, and if it affected his
subsequent actions.

'The only thing that is admissible,' pronounced the
judge, after Jerome's objection, 'is that which was actually
said by the witness to the defendant.'

Delmas nodded gleefully in agreement. 'All that was
said by you,' he told her, 'at that interview.'

He then led Evelyn through the harrowing story of her
seduction at the hands of Stanford White. Tears flowed
from her eyes as she described the final stages and the
jury was visibly affected.

She then described her meeting with Harry Thaw and
how he had accompanied her and her mother to Europe.
She related how, on her return to New York, White had
taken her to see a lawyer who drew up a statement
embodying her supposed story; but according to Evelyn,
she refused to sign it. When she subsequently told Thaw
about all this he became extremely angry and said that
White should be in a penitentiary.

When Jerome rose to cross-examine Evelyn he found
himself confronted by a very determined young woman.
Although she looked extremely nervous and frightened
she still gave a very good account of herself, answering
many of the District Attorney's questions with a simple, 'I
cannot remember,' and not allowing herself to be trapped.

But she was forced to admit that she had received regular sums of money from White when she was going out with Thaw. And even when she went to Europe with Thaw she still used a letter of credit given her by White. And her various affairs with other men were also exposed.

When Jerome produced the affidavit recounting Thaw's ill-treatment of Evelyn when they were in Europe and read out parts of it in court, she denied that she had ever made such an affidavit or signed it, although she admitted the signature looked like hers.

Delmas made his final speech to the jury an impassioned one. He cast Thaw in the role of the chivalrous knight protecting American womanhood – and that his act was justified by the Unwritten Law.

Turning to point to Thaw, who was sitting head in hands at the defence table, he said: 'If that young man is insane then he has a type of insanity which is known to every man who has a family in the length and breadth of the United States. If you want me to give it a name,' he continued, 'I will call it "Dementia Americana", and it is that species of insanity which persuades every American male that any man who comes into his home and defiles his wife puts himself outside the protection of the law.'

The district attorney had a difficult task, hamstrung as he was by his inability to bring rebuttal evidence against Evelyn's version of events, but he wisely decided against an emotional appeal and concentrated instead on attacking the defence case. He poured scorn on the idea of the Unwritten Law, saying that it would have no appeal for an intelligent jury. But he ended on a high note, saying that Evelyn had been playing with the two men. With Thaw she was the wronged woman appealing to his sympathy until he married her. Then, because she knew that he was a philanderer, she kept him in a constant state of jealousy by pursuing an on/off affair with White. And she maintained the architect's interest by complaining that Thaw ill-treated her.

After the judge's summing-up the jury retired. The trial

had been in progress for nearly 2½ months, but Thaw, his family and lawyers looked confident that the verdict would go their way. But the hours dragged by with no decision. It was not until four-thirty the following afternoon that the jury filed back into the courtroom, looking dishevelled and exhausted.

'Have you reached a verdict?' asked the judge.

'Your Honour, we have not,' replied the foreman.

It was later learned that on the final ballot, seven had voted Thaw guilty of first-degree murder and five not guilty by reason of insanity.

A retrial was ordered.

The new trial opened in New York on 6 January 1908 before Judge Dowling. The district attorney again prosecuted, but this time Delphin Delmas was not present in the defence line-up. And gone too was the argument in favour of the Unwritten Law. The new leader of the defence was Martin Littleton, and he stuck firmly to the defence of insanity.

A procession of psychiatrists was paraded to show that Thaw's actions were not those of a sane man. Teachers came forward to state that he had been abnormal even as a child, and even Thaw's mother took the stand to claim that there had been insanity in the family.

The trial dragged on for a month and again it took the jury twenty-four hours to come to a decision. But this time the verdict was: not guilty because of insanity.

Thaw and his family were overjoyed, but their happiness was short-lived.

The judge stated that since it appeared from the evidence that Thaw was liable to a recurrence of attacks of insane violence, his discharge from custody would be a danger to the public: he was therefore to be confined in an institution for the criminally insane.

Within three months Thaw, with the aid of his mother and a new legal staff, applied to be released under a writ of habeas corpus, thus forcing the authorities to justify his continued incarceration. A panel of psychiatrists examined the evidence and debated the question of whether or not he was sane. Not surprisingly, they decided he was insane and he went back to the asylum.

In July of the same year he again applied for a writ of habeas corpus, but again the verdict went against him.

It was not until some four years later that Thaw applied for yet another writ. Yet again, prosecutor Jerome opposed it and the writ was dismissed.

But the following year it appeared that the money and influence behind Thaw had decided on different tactics. In August 1913, with the connivance of one of the warders and a crowd of toughs in two cars, Thaw made his escape from the asylum. He fled to Canada. It took well over a year of legal wrangling to get him back to New York – and at the cost to the authorities of a new trial. Jerome, however, was no longer district attorney and the proceedings went Thaw's way.

In July 1915, he was finally acquitted of all charges and declared legally sane. It had taken the Thaw millions just over seven years to get the verdict reversed and Harry Thaw legally released. A case of justice's not triumphing in the end?

Eighteen months later Thaw was charged with kidnapping and brutally whipping a nineteen-year-old youth. He was judged insane and committed to the mental ward of the Pennsylvania State Hospital.

5   Richard Heming:
Bones in the Barn

It was Midsummer Day in the year 1806. About five o'clock in the evening two farm labourers were walking along a lane near Oddingley, a small village between Worcester and Droitwich and five or six miles from each town.

Suddenly the silence of the quiet evening was broken by the report of a gun. John Lench turned to his companion. 'Someone's out shooting hares,' he said. And Thomas Giles nodded his head in agreement.

But a moment later there came a cry of pain. And someone calling. 'Oh Lord! Oh Lord!'

'It came from over there,' said Giles pointing across a field to his right.

'That's John Barnett's land, isn't it?'

'Either his or the parson's. There's a gate along here.' Giles ran to it and climbed over, closely followed by his companion. The field contained long grass, nearly knee-high, but it looked to be empty. Over to their left they could see a servant girl, driving some cows home for milking, who appeared to be staring at something on the slightly rising ground, beyond the farthest hedge.

As they raced through the long grass they heard more moans coming from beyond the hedge and the sound of thudding blows.

Giles, who was the younger man, outpaced his companion and reached the hedge first. It was tall, but through it he could just make out the shadowy figure of a short man who appeared to be stooping down and pushing a bag into the bottom of the hedge.

'What are you doing?' shouted Giles through the thick mass of foliage.

The man jumped as if surprised by the sound of Giles's voice. 'Nothing,' he muttered. But he dropped the bag and, after trying to peer through the leaves and twigs, turned and ran off across the field.

Lench panted up from behind. 'You go after him,' he gasped out. 'I'll see what's afoot.'

There was a gate a little further along, and Giles climbed over and set off in pursuit. Although the short man was hampered by his long frock-coat, he made surprisingly quick progress over the long grass. But he was no match for the long-legged farm-worker, who rapidly overtook him. Coming up alongside, Giles put out a hand to grasp his shoulder. But sensing Giles's presence, the man leapt away and turned to face his pursuer.

He was hatless and had a high forehead with curly dark brown hair and a jutting black beard, which gave his face a fierce expression. He thrust his hand into the outside pocket of his long blue coat with its white metal buttons.

Don't come any nearer,' he panted. 'I've already shot one man and I'd as soon shoot another!'

Giles took a step backwards. He was brave, but he was not a fool. The gunman could well be telling the truth, and though flintlock pistols had to be reloaded after each shot, the man could easily have another one loaded in his large pocket.

It looked for a moment as if it was going to be a stalemate. But then the assailant began backing away and Giles made no attempt to follow. After a few quick glances over his shoulder the short man suddenly turned and ran towards the next hedge. Giles stood and watched him push his way through the undergrowth and disappear from sight. He would have liked to capture the man, but he contented himself with the thought that the gunman would soon be brought to justice, for Giles had recognized him.

He retraced his steps and soon came across a group of people surrounding someone lying on the ground. Well dressed in the dark clothes of the clergy, a man of about thirty was lying on his side with his legs drawn up against the pain of a belly wound and his hands pressed into his right groin. The whole of that side of his body was drenched with blood. He was moaning softly, but was not really conscious – and this was not surprising, since he had a large cut and bruise over his right eye.

As Giles looked at the man he noticed a curious thing about him: his clothes were smoking.

As if in answer to the unspoken question, Lench turned to Giles. 'The wadding from the pistol,' he whispered; 'it set his clothes alight. And we've only just managed to put the fire out.'

'It's Revd Parker, isn't it?'

'Yes, this is his land,' said Lench, looking round.

A man who had been bending over the injured parson stood up. He was burly and wearing a peasant's smock. Giles recognized him as James Tustin, waggoner to the farmer John Barnett.

Tustin looked across at Giles. 'You went after him. Did you get a good look at him?'

Giles nodded. 'It was Heming the carpenter.'

'The devil it was! Well, he won't get far.'

'I don't know,' said Lench. 'He has some good friends in this district. And I wouldn't be surprised if he wasn't put up to this.'

'That's as maybe,' replied Tustin. Then he conceded. 'The reverend was pretty unpopular with some of the farmers.'

'Don't you think we ought to do something about the

parson?' asked the young milkmaid who had been with the cows. She was nearly in tears.

Tustin shook his head as he looked down at the man on the ground. 'Not much we can do for him, I'm afraid. If you want my opinion he's not long for this world.'

'There must be something we can do,' said the girl, kneeling down beside the wounded man.

'You run and tell the master, Susan. Ask him to send someone for the magistrate at Hadsor. We'll make the reverend as comfortable as we can. Then I'll go and fetch Mrs Parker.'

Susan Surman rose, looked down at her blood-spattered apron and shuddered. Then she went off up the field in the direction of John Barnett's house, a quarter of a mile away.

Giles turned to his friend Lench. 'I think I saw Heming trying to hide something in the hedge.'

Together the two men walked over to the place where they had first seen the assailant.

'This is a bad business,' said Lench, looking back over his shoulder at the bloodstained form lying on the grass. 'He may have been a bit young and impetuous,' continued Lench, 'but there was no cause to threaten him like some of these farmers did.'

Giles said nothing. Sometimes, he felt, it was better for labourers not to get involved in controversy with the big farmers in the district. For if you made yourself unpopular and lost your job there was only the dead-end of parish relief.

They reached the hedge and almost immediately saw the brown leather bag discarded by the fleeing gunman. Lench bent down and picked it up. Inside was an old flintlock pistol which had obviously been fired recently, for the barrel was still warm. But the butt was broken off almost up to the lock and the shattered end was bloodstained.

'He fired at the parson,' surmised Lench. 'Then, when

the poor man began to shout and cry for help, beat him over the head with the pistol.'

Some time later Revd Reginald Pyndar rode up on his horse. He was a middle-aged man, a local magistrate who lived at Hadsor, a village near Droitwich. After dismounting, he stood for a while looking down at the weeping figure of the parson's wife, kneeling beside her husband. Then he stooped and gently raised her to her feet. After comforting the sobbing woman he took her place beside his friend and fellow clergyman. He took the young man's hand in his.

'George,' he said, 'do you know who did this?'

But a faint bubbling of pinkish froth from the dying man's lips was the only response.

After some time Revd Pyndar stood up and brushed a tear from his eye. He crossed himself.

'He's gone to Jesus. I'll say a prayer for him now, then someone can fetch a chair so we can carry him. We'll take him to the vicarage.'

After the prayer, Tustin went to get a chair and while he was away Pyndar began quietly to question those who remained near the body. Then he got back on his horse and rode over to the Barnett farmhouse. As he entered the farmyard he saw Susan Surman crossing to the cowshed with a pail in her hand.

He leaned down and said: 'Susan. Is John Barnett in?'

'Yes sir.'

The magistrate got down from his horse and knocked on the kitchen door. It was opened by an elderly lady whom he recognized as the widow Barnett.

Pyndar took his hat off. 'Good evening, Mrs Barnett. Could I speak to John?'

'My son's not in. And I don't know when he'll be back.' She shut the door in his face.

Revd Pyndar was used to a certain lack of manners among some country folk and, merely shrugging his shoulders, he walked back to his horse. Then on an impulse he went to the cowshed door.

'You misinformed me, girl. I've been told that Mr Barnett is not at home.'

Susan looked up from her milking. 'Mr William Barnett may not be home, sir. I don't know if he's back yet from Bromsgrove Fair. But the other brother, Mr John Barnett, certainly is. He leaned out of the parlour window some time ago to tell me to get on with the milking.'

Revd Pyndar retraced his steps and banged on the door with the end of his riding crop. This time it was answered by a servant, and the reverend pushed passed her and entered the house. A few moments later he emerged with his arm in a fatherly fashion about the shoulders of a man in his thirties. He was a well-set-up young man, but had a sulky look on his face.

Just at that moment they both saw the group carrying the chair, with the body of Revd Parker on it, going by in the fields just beyond the farmhouse.

'What do you know about that, John?' asked Pyndar, indicating the mourning group with a wave of his hand.

'Nothing at all,' came the surly reply.

'Now, that surprises me, John. For I seem to remember a famous occasion a few years ago when you were abusive towards Revd Parker and went so far as to kick him.'

'I don't remember that.'

'You should, because you were taken to court for assault – and were fined, if I recall it correctly.'

There was no reply from the stubborn young man.

'And that's not all, is it? You and your farming friends have been abusing the parson for years about the way he collects his tythes.'

This served to stir John Barnett. 'We just can't afford to simply give away butter and eggs and all the rest to the Church,' he snapped.

'A lot of it goes to the poor, you know, John. But leave that aside for the moment. There's something else I seem to recall. Just this last Easter, wasn't there a parish meeting in the church?'

'There usually is.'

'Yes, but wasn't this an especially acrimonious one? Didn't Revd Parker complain about overspending on the dinner which takes place after the meeting? And weren't you and some of your friends so incensed with this that at the actual dinner, which he didn't attend, you proposed a toast to the "Buonaparte of Oddingley". And wasn't the toast drunk with the left hand, to signify an even greater insult?'

'It doesn't mean to say that I'd kill him, though.'

'Oh, I'm not saying that you shot the reverend. I believe we know who did that. I was talking to some people down in the fields just now and one of them actually caught sight of a man running away after trying to hide a gun under the hedge. He said it was a man called Heming, Richard Heming, who lives in Droitwich – a carpenter and wheelwright. Do you know him?'

'I may have seen him about.'

'I should think you may! Susan Surman told me earlier that she's seen this Heming hanging about in one of your fields – the one next to Revd Parker's field, where he was shot – every morning and evening for the past fortnight.'

'I think I have heard her mention it.'

'I think you might have done, since she tells me you teased her, saying he was her boyfriend.'

John Barnett scowled. 'All this doesn't prove I had anything to do with the parson getting shot.'

'No. It's not evidence that would be accepted in court. But I'm going to have a search instituted for this Heming this very evening, before it gets dark. We'll also be searching your house as well as some others. Your man Tustin says he knows Heming by sight so he will be a useful man to have on the hunt. And when we catch him – and I have little doubt that we will – then perhaps he'll be able to tell us why he shot Revd Parker. And if anybody paid him to do it.' And with that he mounted his horse and rode off, leaving the young farmer staring after him.

Tustin, the waggoner, was quite ready to lead the hunt for Heming, but unaccountably there seemed to be a lot of work for him to do around the farm that evening and he didn't have time to go. Nevertheless, a search was instituted. The countryside was scoured until it got too dark to see properly, and then the search was continued the next day. But the hunt turned up nothing. A few days later a search of all the farmhouses, barns and cowsheds in the area met with no greater success.

On the day following the murder the local coroner, Mr Barnaby, held an inquest. It was established that Heming had left his home in Droitwich early on the day of the murder to go and work on the farm of Captain Evans in Oddingley. He had worked there, helping to pull poles out of the horse pond, until about half-past four, when he had left. Nothing more was seen of him until after the murder.

The jury brought in a verdict of 'wilful murder by some person or persons at present unknown'. However, the description given by Giles, and the fact that Heming was subsequently missing from the neighbourhood, was enough for the local magistrates to offer a reward of fifty guineas for his capture.

Days passed, however, and there was no sighting of Heming. Even the handsome reward brought no clues and it seemed that the man had successfully got away. Weeks stretched into months and still there was no news of him; most people came to believe that he would never be found. Indeed, after some years a rumour began circulating in the village that Heming had gone to North America.

Two years after the murder, in July 1808, a curious incident occurred. A Mr John Roe, licensee of the New Inn, Inkberrow, a village some ten miles from Oddingley, went to the magistrates in Droitwich and made a deposition.

He said that just before the murder of Revd Parker he had been travelling to the market in Bromsgrove. He stopped for a drink at the White Hare in Droitwich and saw a man he knew, James Taylor, who was a farrier. Taylor came over to talk to him and, after sipping his beer and looking all round the room to see if he was observed, leaned across the table towards him.

'Roe, do you want to earn yourself fifty pounds?'

'Who do I have to kill?' asked Roe with a smile.

But his joke met with a surprising response. Again the blacksmith looked over his shoulder, this time with more alarm. 'Keep your voice down.'

Roe's mouth fell open. 'You're not serious?'

Taylor nodded his head. 'The money has already been collected,' he said in a low voice, adding hurriedly, 'I'm just the messenger.'

'Well, who has the money?'

'Do you know Thomas Clewes?'

Roe nodded. 'Farms at Oddingley.'

'Netherwood, close by.'

Roe nodded his head again. 'Who else is involved in this?'

'I can't say.'

'Clewes wouldn't have fifty pounds to give to anybody,' mused Roe. 'He's not a wealthy man. If there is money of that kind on offer I would guess it comes from Captain Evans and possibly the Barnett brothers.'

Taylor jerked his head impatiently. 'Well, will you do it?' He looked round the room again and lowered his voice still further. 'We can supply the gun.'

'Who is it to be?'

Taylor leaned up close and mouthed the words rather than spoke them: 'Revd Parker.'

'I'll have to think it over.'

Roe continued his journey to the Bromsgrove market and, on his return through Droitwich as he was passing the White Hare again, Taylor came running out and caught him by the arm. He had obviously been in the pub all day and was none too steady on his feet.

'Are you going to help us?' Taylor slurred.

Roe shook him off. By this time he had thought things over. 'No, I'm not. I wouldn't be associated with anything like that.' And he went on his way.

Roe's deposition before Revd Pyndar, however, had nothing to support it. James Taylor had worked for many farmers in the district. And like most blacksmiths of the day he also performed veterinary services, such as bloodletting operations on horses and cattle and the slaughter of diseased farm animals. He also had an unsavoury reputation, having been accused some years before of stealing Church plate. But he hotly denied Roe's charges and there was no real evidence to connect him, or any of the other people mentioned by Roe, with the murder of the parson.

There the matter rested until nearly a quarter of a century later. Then, on 21 January 1830, Charles Burton was removing the foundations of an old barn near Oddingley when he came across some bones, a pair of shoes and an old carpenter's rule. This may not seem much. A man doing such a job could expect to turn up all kinds of rubbish. But Burton was the brother-in-law of the missing Richard Heming, and he knew all about the murder case.

He stopped work immediately and covered up the finds he had made, in case anyone else should come across them; then went to Droitwich and saw Revd Pyndar, who was now quite elderly, but still one of the local magistrates.

'I've found Richard Heming!' he blurted.

'You did very well, Burton,' said Pyndar when the man had finished his story, 'especially covering up the remains and coming directly to me. We don't want anyone else to know of this discovery until we can arrange for it to be properly investigated. Will you go back to the barn and keep watch? Make sure no one else disturbs anything? I will see Mr Smith, the coroner, and report the find to him. Then we'll arrange for a surgeon to be present when the body is disinterred.'

The next day a small party gathered round the spot where Burton had discovered the shoes. In addition to himself there was Mr Smith, a local solicitor, who was the coroner for the district, Mr Pierpoint, a surgeon, and Pyndar.

The barn had been a large one with double doors at either end. One end of it was quite near the farmhouse and the other close to the Oddingley–Crowle road. On one side, there was a pond and it was here in what had been a double bay, close to the end wall, that the shoes had been found.

Mr Pierpoint carefully scraped away the earth and soon off-white bones appeared in the powdery soil. Eventually a complete skeleton was unearthed with pieces of clothing still adhering to some of the bones.

The shoes were identified as belonging to Heming by his brother-in-law. The carpenter's rule had been found close to one of the thigh-bones, and Burton confirmed that Heming always carried a rule in a special pocket in his coat.

Pierpoint measured the skeleton, whose length showed it to belong to a short man, which Heming was. The skeleton was discovered on its left side, and since the shoes still contained the bones of the feet, it was safe to assume that the body had been buried still clothed. The skull confirmed that Heming himself had been murdered. It had been literally smashed to pieces, obviously by a blow, or several blows, from a blunt instrument.

'I suppose you can't tell me how long those bones have been there?' asked Mr Smith of Pierpoint.

The surgeon shook his head. 'A good many years, is all I can say.'

While Pierpoint collected together the bones into a box

along with other items discovered in the grave, Pyndar drew Burton to one side.

'Do you recall who owned this barn back in 1806?'

Burton nodded his head. 'The same man who owned the rest of Netherwood Farm in those days. Mr Thomas Clewes.'

Pyndar located Clewes in a small cottage in the village of Oddingley. The man was now in considerably reduced circumstances, having failed as a farmer some years before. He was sitting by the fire, broodily smoking a pipe.

Pyndar came right to the point. 'We've just dug up a skeleton in that barn you used to own at Netherwood.'

The effect of his words was all he could have hoped for. The pipe fell out of Clewes's mouth and clattered to the floor as he jumped to his feet. His face went pale and he began to tremble.

Pyndar calmly brushed the dust from his coat and sat down on a nearby chair. All this without looking at Clewes again. He wanted to give his words time to sink in. Then he looked up at the trembling man. 'We've very good reason to believe that the skeleton belongs to a certain Richard Heming, who disappeared soon after the murder of Revd Parker.' He paused again. Then said quietly, but with emphasis, 'You'd better tell me just what happened, Clewes.'

The ex-farmer made a desperate effort to control himself. He gulped and passed his tongue over dry lips. He said nothing for some time, then when his words came they were half strangled in his throat. 'I don't know anything about it.'

'Come on, Clewes. That's not good enough. A man is buried in your barn and you say you don't know anything about it? That's ridiculous!'

Clewes made another effort at self-control. He gulped again and cleared his throat. 'I haven't owned that barn at Netherwood for fifteen years or more. I was forced to give up the farm in 1816 or thereabouts. If a man was found there it's nothing to do with me.'

Pyndar stood up and faced the ex-farmer with a grim expression. 'You got away with it all those years ago, merely because we didn't know what had happened to Heming. But now we know – don't think you'll escape justice a second time!'

He remounted his horse and rode out to Sale Green, a little village only a mile and a half from Oddingley. After making some enquiries he located a man who had been a cobbler at the time of Revd Parker's murder, but who had now retired.

'Well sir,' said the cobbler, after Pyndar had told him of the situation, 'I gave my evidence at the inquest on the death of the parson, as you know. But I'll gladly repeat it. Let me see now, Revd Parker often used to come into my shop for a chat. And one day not long before he was killed we were talking, when he looked out of the window and saw Thomas Clewes coming. "I don't want to meet Clewes," says he, and left by the back way, after bidding me good-morning.

'In comes Clewes at the front door. All swagger and dash as usual. "Was that the parson I saw sneaking out the back?" he says. "Good riddance to him, I say. I only wish we could be rid of him for ever." He leaned over the counter towards me. "There's fifty pounds for any man as will shoot the parson!" '.

The next day Revd Pyndar talked to John Perkins, another who had been a prosperous farmer at the time of the murder, but was now only a farm labourer. He remembered a morning when he had been visiting Captain Evans. News was given the captain that one of Revd Parker's servants had called about the tythes. The ex-soldier flew into a rage at once and began cursing the parson.

'Damn him!' he shouted. 'There's no more harm shooting him than there is a mad dog.'

'Mind you,' continued Perkins, 'that was typical of the

captain. Although he was over seventy at the time he was still a violent man. He would shout and curse at almost everybody when he felt like it. Even the young lad George Banks, who used to work for him and who some thought was his illegitimate son, couldn't appease him at times.'

'Didn't his sister also work for Captain Evans?'

'That's right, sir, Miss Catherine Banks was the old chap's housekeeper.'

'How old was the captain when he died?' asked Pyndar.

'They say he was well over ninety. He retired from the 89th Foot on half pay, you know, a long time before the war.'

'Yes, I know,' said Pyndar. 'He was a magistrate at Droitwich for many years.'

Due to the efforts of Revd Pyndar in collecting witnesses, the coroner was able to open the inquest on the remains discovered in the barn at the Talbot Inn, near Worcester, at ten o'clock on Tuesday, 26 January 1830.

The coroner heard the evidence of Charles Burton, M. Pierpoint and Elizabeth Newberry, who at the time of the parson's murder had been Heming's wife. She identified as Heming's the rule found in the barn, a pocket knife also found there and the shoes.

The rest of the first day was taken up with witnesses proving that Clewes had been the owner of the barn, that he had threatened the parson on numerous occasions and had been seen in intimate conversation with Heming at various times prior to the murder.

At the end of the second day the foreman of the jury, William Bass, made a deposition before a county magistrate, stating that the jury believed that Thomas Clewes had a guilty knowledge of the murder of Richard Heming and that the purposes of public justice would be furthered by the commitment to prison of the former for further examination. Accordingly, Clewes was taken by two constables to the county gaol.

Over the weekend in prison Clewes finally made a

confession and the inquest jury was called to the prison to hear it.

According to Clewes Revd Parker was shot on Bromsgrove Fair day. Early the next morning, George Banks approached him in the fields.

'We've got Heming at our house,' he said (meaning the house of Captain Evans), 'and we don't know what to do with him. Will you help us out and let him come down here?'

'No, I won't. I don't want anything to do with him.' And Clewes turned away and walked off. Banks, after muttering to himself, went away.

Clewes had to go into Oddingley later in the morning and as he was walking by Captain Evans's house he saw the old soldier in his garden. The captain called out. 'Come into the field, will you?'

Clewes obediently turned off the road into the captain's field, in which they were shielded by the hedgerows and could not be seen from the road or the garden.

'I've had Heming at my house this morning,' said the captain. 'And something must be done about him. I ordered him to go down to your place, get into your barn and keep out of sight in the daytime. We shall have to do something by him. I'll come down to your house tonight and bring somebody with me. We must give the poor devil some money and send him off. Will you come to the barn at eleven o'clock tonight? It won't take long.'

'I don't want to be involved in any way.'

'Come on. It won't make any difference to you. You must come, otherwise all your dogs will start barking and cause a commotion when we get there, and it may all come out.'

Clewes realized that he was trapped with the others. He reluctantly agreed and, just as the clock was striking eleven, let himself out of the back door and crept across to the barn. Although it was late it was still not fully dark and he easily recognized the three men standing by the barn door. There was Captain Evans and George Banks, who was wearing a peasant's smock, and the farrier, James Taylor.

Clewes opened the barn door and they crept inside. Here it was much darker, but the captain produced a dim lantern, whose low light showed up the bays of the barn on each side.

'Hullo, Heming,' called the captain in a low voice. 'Are you there?'

There came a rustling from the other end of the barn and all four men walked towards it.

'Here, sir,' came a muffled voice from under some straw at the furthest end.

'Get up, Heming,' said the captain. 'I've got some meat for you.'

There was a pile of straw about knee-high and to one side of it some loose hay. It was in this that Heming had concealed himself, for they could see it moving as he struggled to get up. Captain Evans, holding the lantern, and James Taylor jumped up on to the pile of straw. Clewes and Banks remained standing on the paved part of the barn, the threshing floor.

In the flickering light of the lantern the short stocky figure of Heming emerged from the straw in which he had been hiding. As he came upright, Taylor took from his pocket what looked like a short club. It was a blood-stick (sometimes called a fleam-knocker) – a stick about ten inches long, made of box, yew or other hardwood with a kind of knob at one end, sometimes covered in lead. It was used to tap the end of the fleam or lancet, in bleeding operations, to enable it to penetrate the tough skin of a horse. A swift sharp blow was said to cause the animal the minimum of distress.

Taylor brought the end of the blood-stick down hard on the unsuspecting Heming's head – then followed it with two or three more crushing blows. Heming collapsed with a low moan on the floor and after twitching for a while lay still.

'That'll do for him,' said the captain, with satisfaction.

'If I'd known you were going to do that,' cried Clewes, 'I wouldn't have come.'

But the old soldier took no notice of him as he and Taylor came down off the pile of straw.

'What's to be done with him now?' asked the farrier.

'We daren't take him out of doors, blast him,' said the captain; 'somebody might see us.'

Taylor nodded in understanding and left the barn, reappearing in a few moments with a spade.

'We'll soon put him safe, don't you worry,' said the captain to Clewes.

Taylor went to an unpaved part near the end wall of the barn, where the earth was reasonably loose. He began to dig, while the captain held the lantern. After he had dug out a shallow trench, he and the captain dragged the body over to the grave and tipped it in. Taylor then refilled the hole.

When the farrier had finished, the old soldier turned to Clewes. 'You can have anything you want. But don't you damn well tell anyone what has happened here tonight.'

And after that they went their separate ways. When Clewes got back into his house he found that the whole episode had taken no more than half an hour.

The next day he went to Pershore Fair. Late in the afternoon he recognized George Banks and John Barnett. They were both carrying small parcels. Banks turned to Clewes as he came up and handed him a parcel. 'Here's some money. It's what Heming was to have had. Mind you keep silent and tell nobody what you've seen.'

Barnett also handed Clewes a parcel, but said nothing.

When he got home later Clewes opened the parcels and discovered they contained together twenty-six pounds in notes.

The next day Clewes received a message requesting him to go and see Captain Evans. The old soldier gave him five pounds with the words: 'You can have this amount any time you want, provided you remember to keep silent.'

Later the same day the captain's housekeeper, Miss Catherine Banks, George's sister, met Clewes in a corridor of the captain's house and fell on her knees before him. She gripped his coat with both hands.

'Please, please, Thomas, promise that you will never say a word. I don't know what has been going on, but I'm afraid the captain and young George have been doing bad things. I'm so afraid that if you speak someone will come to be hanged. Promise, promise, you will say nothing!'

Clewes promised.

A few days after this the captain suggested that Clewes haul some loads of marl, a kind of loam often used at the time to make hard flooring, into the barn to cover the spot where Heming had been buried. This Clewes did.

After hearing the confession and some more witnesses the jury brought in a verdict of wilful murder against Clewes and George Banks, and John Barnett was found to be an accessory before the fact. Those were the only members of the conspiracy who were alive at the time, since Captain Evans had died in May 1829 and James Taylor in 1816.

The trial of Thomas Clewes began on Saturday, 13 March 1830, at Worcester, before Mr Justice Littledale. It was essentially a re-run of the inquest. The same large number of witnesses was heard and the confession of Clewes was read by prosecuting counsel, Mr Curwood.

When the judge began his summing-up, however, he pointed out to the jury that even with the large number of witnesses brought by the prosecution there was no direct evidence either to confirm or deny the confession. And the jury must either accept the whole of it or reject it. And if they accepted the story, then in his opinion there were not sufficient grounds for convicting Clewes of being a principal in the murder of Heming.

The jury took his advice and brought in a verdict of not guilty.

Mr Curwood then rose to his feet and said that in view

of the verdict on Clewes, and since there was even less
evidence against Banks and Barnett, he did not propose to
call any evidence against them. And they were
accordingly acquitted.

6 Stephanus Louis van Wyk: Killer of the Veld

The car drew up outside the half-completed house in Claremont, a suburb of Johannesburg in South Africa. At that time, June 1928, the area was under development as a new housing estate, but there were still only a few houses dotted about the largely open veld. The passenger door of the car opened and a tall man stepped out, to be followed, from the driver's side, by a shorter man. Both began to walk towards the house, on which builders were working.

The tall man was carrying a black hat in his hand, for although this was winter in South Africa it was still a very sunny day. He was only thirty-eight years old, but his bald pate shone in the sunshine and his heavy moustache, much favoured by South African farmers in the 1920s, made him look older. He was wearing dark, sober clothes and the expression on his face – indeed his whole demeanour – bespoke the strongly religious Dutch stock from which he came.

'If you'll allow me to do the talking, Mr Whyte,' he said. 'You can't be too careful when it comes to dealing with the natives around here, and even with some of the white men.' He gazed up at the single white man working up on scaffolding at the side of the house. 'It doesn't do to be too familiar.'

'Oh, I agree entirely, Mr van Wyk,' said the smaller

man. 'It certainly looks as if you are going to have a nice place here in a few weeks.'

'Provided I can keep them all at it. But you know what workmen are like these days.' He looked up again at the white man on the scaffolding. 'Don't bother to come down, Mr Marais,' he called. 'We can show ourselves around. This is Mr Whyte, by the way.' He pointed to the shorter man at his side. 'He's an estate agent.'

Mr Marais nodded his head and watched as van Wyk showed Whyte round the property. They picked their way between piles of bricks and rubble, and van Wyk led the estate agent into all the rooms on the ground floor. Then he could be seen pointing out the limits of the plot. Eventually he turned and waved at Marais as together he and the estate agent began to walk back to the car.

'Well then, what do you think, Mr Whyte?'

'I think we can arrange that £400 bond for you. You've shown me the plans of your house, which you're going to use as security, and now I've seen round, it looks quite satisfactory.'

'When it's complete it's going to be worth at least £800.'

'Yes, I think it will.'

'When do you think you'll be able to let me have the money?' asked van Wyk. 'I need it to buy some more building materials, you see.'

The estate agent thought for a moment. 'I should be able to let you have a little next week.'

'And the balance the week after? I need to meet a number of commitments to do with the house.'

'I think we might manage that,' replied Whyte cautiously. 'Repayments will have to start fairly soon though.'

'That won't be a problem.'

The two continued their walk to the car, watched by Marais on the scaffolding. He was, in fact, the present owner of the house, which he was building with his own workmen. He knew van Wyk, who was also a local builder and moneylender, and who owned the empty plot next door. He had been amused at van Wyk's interest in the house, even going so far as to lend him the plans. And now when the man turned up with an estate agent, Marais assumed that van Wyk was showing the man what his own house would look like when it was finished.

But William Whyte never saw any more of the £400 he advanced van Wyk, and after waiting some time for the promised repayments to arrive, he went to the address he had for the man, but found him absent. Whyte went to the police.

They soon discovered that there were quite a number of estate agents and solicitors in the Johannesburg area who had been hoodwinked by the crafty van Wyk, parting with sums ranging from £350 to £400. In every case he used as security houses on the Claremont estate which he didn't own.

Meanwhile van Wyk had gone to Bloemfontein, a city some 260 miles to the south-west. There he took up residence with his wife and two children in the suburb of Erfenis.

Stephanus Louis van Wyk had been born on a farm called Waterval near Trompsburg, about 75 miles to the south-west of Bloemfontein, and had spent a large part of his early life there. He had numerous relatives who lived in the vicinity.

Early in January 1929 he met one of these, Johan Moller, a 28-year-old clerk at the Bloemfontein Supreme Court, outside the post office in the city.

Moller was van Wyk's nephew and the two men spoke together in Afrikaans.

'Glad I've run in to you, Uncle Faan,' said Moller. 'Do you know the police are looking for you?'

Van Wyk looked uneasy, but said nothing.

'It's true,' said Moller, 'I've seen a warrant sworn out for your arrest on a charge of fraud.'

'It's all a mistake,' muttered van Wyk, 'over a slight error I made in connection with some bonds I passed.'

'I'm sure it is, Uncle,' said Moller cheerfully, 'but there's a warrant out just the same.'

'You won't tell them you've seen me, will you, Takkie?'

'Of course not! I'm your friend, aren't I? And if you want any help or advice … Anything I can do for you and Auntie Hessie … You know I will.'

The tall figure of van Wyk stood pensively for a moment. 'Jesus will reward you,' he said almost absent-mindedly. Then he gazed down at his young companion. 'If there's going to be trouble I could do with a good lawyer.'

'Nothing simpler. I'll find you a first-class man.'

'I shall have to get away, but I want someone to look after Hessie and the children. I could send her to stay with my brother. But it's a long way … I'd be prepared to pay, of course.'

'Don't worry about it,' said Moller quickly. 'I'll look after her. That is if, er, if anything happens to you. I'll use my own money.'

'There's no need for that,' said van Wyk sharply. 'The Lord helps him who helps himself. If you come round to my home tonight, I'll give you some money for her.'

'Can't manage tonight, I'm afraid Uncle, but I'll come tomorrow, in my lunch hour.'

The next day Johan Moller arrived at the house in Erfenis at about midday. Van Wyk drew him to one side. 'Let's go into the garden. I don't want to talk in front of Hessie – she gets so worried about things.'

They strolled in the garden behind the house.

'I've found you a lawyer, Uncle,' remarked the young man. 'A Mr Ramsbottom. He's very good. But don't worry yourself about his fee. I'll take care of that. I've a few pounds put away.'

'You'll get your reward in Heaven, Takkie. Of that I'm sure.' The older man seized and pressed the hands of the younger.

Moller was embarrassed and withdrew his hands. 'I'll also look after Auntie Hessie for you.'

All at once van Wyk became businesslike. He looked around to make sure that he wasn't being observed from the windows of the house behind him. Then slipped his hand into the inside pocket of his coat and withdrew a thick wad of notes. 'There's £850 there, Takkie. Take it and put it away quickly.'

The young man fumbled the bulky bundle into his inside pocket.

'Now listen carefully,' continued van Wyk. 'I've got a bag packed in the house and I'm going to slip away in a few minutes. But just in case anything goes wrong and I'm picked up, keep that money safe and don't tell anyone you've got it. They will undoubtedly try and make me bankrupt, and any money the authorities can get hold of will go to my creditors, so I want you to keep that money out of sight.'

'Of course, Uncle, you can rely on me.'

'You can also use part of it for looking after Hessie and the children, paying the advocate and getting me out on bail. If anyone asks, say the money is yours.'

The young man nodded his head. 'You're putting a lot of trust in me, Uncle. I shall try and live up to it.'

For a fraction of a second a look of doubt appeared on van Wyk's face, but then it disappeared. 'I must be off, now Takkie.'

'You wouldn't like us to pray together? Just before you go?'

'Of course, Takkie.'

They knelt together on the grass and it was while they were so engaged that the police appeared. One at the back door of the house, another at the garden gate just to make sure van Wyk didn't make his escape that way. He went quietly.

Van Wyk was taken under escort to Johannesburg and appeared before the magistrates there on a charge of fraud.

Mr Ramsbottom, the advocate sent by Moller, interviewed van Wyk; but it turned out that the lawyer was also involved in the sequestration proceedings against van Wyk's estate and therefore could not represent him. Van Wyk conducted his own defence. But he was found guilty, admitted a previous conviction for theft, and was sent to prison in Pretoria.

During his stay in prison the hoped-for assistance from Moller did not materialize. The young man did write to the trustees of van Wyk's insolvent estate asking if they could spare something from the estate for Mrs van Wyk and her children, but they replied that they could not. They sent him £11, however, which had been found in the con man's pockets when he was arrested. Moller passed on only £3. After Mrs van Wyk had complained to her husband in jail he wrote to the trustees and they persuaded a reluctant Moller to return the £8, which they then passed on to Mrs van Wyk, who by this time was staying with her brother-in-law at Beyersberg, in the Philippolis district.

Van Wyk was released from prison on Saturday, 5 July 1930, and the following Saturday arrived in Bloemfontein by train. He arrived at the home of Hendric Truter, a park superintendent with whom Moller lodged, at one o'clock and was shown up to the young man's room. Moller was lying on the bed. He had been expecting his uncle to call, but he still got up rather nervously when van Wyk appeared at the door.

'Did you get my letter, Takkie?' asked van Wyk.

'Yes. I can explain about the money. I still have it all, but it'll take me a day or two to get hold of it, because I put it away for safe-keeping.'

'Well, I shall expect a full account in due course, but for the moment that's not what I'm here for. I need your help.'

'Of course, Uncle, you can count on me.'

'How do you fancy a trip to Trompsburg?' He paused, smiling one of his rare smiles at the young man's look of mystification. 'We shall need your car, and a pick and shovel. Now listen, I've never told anyone else about this before.' He quietly went to the door, opened it and took a good look along the landing. Then he came back and sat on the end of the bed. When he did speak, his voice was so low that Moller had to crane his head to hear him. 'Just before I was arrested I went secretly one night to Waterval. I took £3,000 in notes with me in a box and buried it in a jackal hole, under a large stone, on a remote part of the farm. It'll never be found unless I dig it up again.'

For a moment a gleam appeared in the young man's eyes. Then it was gone and was replaced by a serious look on his face. 'But do you think you'll be able to locate the spot again?'

'Of course I will,' said van Wyk impatiently. 'I know the place like a shepherd knows the faces of his sheep. Now here's what I suggest we do. We don't want to be seen together too much, so I'll leave now. You see if you can get hold of a pick and shovel, then pick me up in your car at the corner of the street. Can you do that?' The young man nodded. 'We'll drive down to Waterval. It should be dark by the time we get there, so we'll not easily be seen on the farm. I'll locate the spot and we'll dig up the money. Again, I don't think we ought to be seen together. So you could get a train back to Bloemfontein and I could take the car and go on to Beyersberg to see Hessie and the children.'

'What are we going to do about the money? Do you think it's safe for you to be carrying large sums of money around. If you're stopped by the police how will you explain it?'

Van Wyk scratched his chin. 'That's a point. Perhaps you'd better bring the money back with you.'

Moller found his landlord by the tennis courts, in the park he managed, and asked if he could borrow a pick and shovel. He was directed by Truter to have a word with the boy in charge of the stores. The park superintendent saw Moller drive away with the implements at about two o'clock.

About seven o'clock the next morning van Wyk appeared at the front door of the Beamish homestead, in the Trompsburg area. He looked dishevelled and dirty and his eyes were red with lack of sleep. Nevertheless Arthur Beamish recognized him. The tall van Wyk explained that his car was stuck, up on the road, about a mile away. Arthur Beamish sent his two sons, Charles and young Arthur, who was only fourteen, with the older man to help start the car.

When they approached the vehicle, a dark blue 1925 Chevrolet, Charles said, 'Have you got the car keys?'

The older man fumbled in his pockets for some time. 'Do you know, I've lost them. Must have dropped them on the way up to your homestead.'

'Well, have you got a penknife? You can sometimes start these with a small blade.'

Van Wyk produced a small penknife, but the blade was still too large to fit into the ignition. Charles filed it down and they eventually managed to get the car started. Van Wyk drove the two brothers back to their homestead, then went on his way.

After van Wyk had gone, Charles began to retrace his steps back to where the car had been. He'd noticed something odd on the way home. About 500 yards from where the car had broken down was a small pond, and there was something sticking up out of the water. When he drew near he saw that it was the handle of a spade or shovel. Someone had obviously tossed the implement into the water the previous night, for it hadn't been there the day before.

Charles approached the pond edge carefully. He'd lived on the veld all his life and was experienced at studying the tracks of animals and man. In the mud at the edge of the pond could clearly be seen a man's footprints. But it was equally plain that whereas one of his feet had had a boot on it, the other had not.

Young Arthur Beamish also made a discovery that day. Not very far from where the shovel was discovered he saw what proved to be the handle of a pickaxe jutting out from another pool.

Later the same day van Wyk called at Waterval and saw his brother-in-law, Mr L.B. Grobbelaar, the owner of the farm. Van Wyk announced that he was going for a walk on the farm. Borrowing a stick, but refusing the offer of company, he set off in the direction of the farm windmill.

When he returned, sometime later, he journeyed on to Bloemfontein where he stopped the night with some friends. The next morning van Wyk called on another friend in the city, Louis van Selm.

'Louis, I want you to set up a meeting with my creditors so I can pay them what I owe.'

His friend laughed. 'Where are you going to get the money to do that, Stephan?'

'Quite a lot of people owe me money, notably Johan Moller, who has £850 of mine.'

Van Selm looked at van Wyk in a speculative manner. 'Did you know he's missing?' he asked.

'No, I didn't.'

'Hasn't been in to work since Saturday, apparently. Left his lodgings in his car on Saturday afternoon, with a pick and shovel, and nobody's seen him since. His mother's getting very worried about him and is thinking of going to the police.'

'I wouldn't advise her to do that. If he turns up in a few days, as I'm sure he will, she's going to look pretty foolish.'

Van Selm carefully examined his fingernails. 'I heard that you went to see him on Saturday?' he aked quietly.

'Well, yes, that's right. He's got all this money of mine and I went to see him about it. But he said he'd get it for me in a few days and I left.'

After another silence, van Selm remarked casually. 'And yet you've been seen driving his car.'

'It's not his car,' snapped van Wyk. 'It's mine. I wrote to him when I was in prison asking him to buy me a car. It's the least he could do after all the money he owes me. Look, Louis, I've got to go to Johannesburg for a few days, but I'll be back next Wednesday. Will you call a creditors' meeting for that day? I'll meet them and pay them what I've managed to collect.'

Van Selm duly set up the meeting, but van Wyk never appeared.

On the very day that van Wyk had his meeting with van Selm, Sergeant T.A. du Plessis of the Bloemfontein CID received a report of the disappearance of Johan Moller and began his investigations. It didn't take him very long to put together the pieces of the puzzle: Moller's connection with van Wyk; the latter's appearance at Moller's lodgings on the Saturday; the departure of the young man in his car; and the subsequent sightings of van Wyk at Trompsburg.

Du Plessis left for Trompsburg on 18 July and the following day visited several farms in the area. In the company of Sergeant Burger and Constable Goosen of the local police force, he arrived at Waterval and saw Mr Grobbelaar. After some discussion they decided to search the homestead, and the farmer went with them.

He led them away across the veld towards the windmill, explaining that this was the way van Wyk had gone on his walk. When they'd reached the windmill he looked around and said, 'Over there, towards the road, there's a sandy area, easy to dig, near some jackal holes.'

They walked in that direction and eventually came across a couple of shallow pits. 'Last May,' said Grobbelaar, 'we dug these two down to about five or six feet to get at the jackals – but then refilled them. As you can see the soil has settled a bit in each of them.'

In one of the pits, however, the earth looked as if it had

recently been disturbed. 'We'll try that one,' said du Plessis.

They began to remove the soil carefully and had gone only a couple of feet down when they felt something hard below the surface. Continuing to scrape away the earth, they soon saw the sole of a shoe.

When the body was finally removed, in the presence of the district surgeon of Trompsburg and a local magistrate, it was discovered to be fully clothed and lying in a huddled position, head downwards. There was a considerable amount of blood on the head and in the surrounding soil.

In the back of the jacket there was a hole, which penetrated the waistcoat, shirt and even, to a depth of an inch or so, the body.

Sergeant du Plessis discovered a wristwatch on the body which had stopped at 10.20, a ring engraved 'Takkie' and, in the hip pocket, car keys which were found to fit the dark blue Chevrolet. The clothes were not torn or disturbed, except for the hole in the back; but two buttons at the back of the trousers had been torn off and were found in the burial pit.

Du Plessis also took possession of the pick and shovel discovered on the Beamish farm and made plaster casts of the footprints found near the ponds. Subsequently, the Trompsburg police found a pair of socks, in the same locale marked 'S.van W'.

Dr Rauch, the district surgeon of Trompsburg, conducted the post-mortem. He revealed that death had been caused by haemorrhage and compression of the brain owing to fractures of the skull. The several fissured fractures on the vault of the skull appeared to have been caused by a blow from a spade, shovel or some other blunt instrument such as the socket of a pick.

The puncture wound in the back was about an inch to the left of the spine and it penetrated the spinal muscles to a depth of about an inch. Not enough to seriously disable a normal healthy man. And it could have been caused by the sharp end of a pick.

The body was soon identified as that of Johan Moller.

The police theory, which formed the basis of the prosecution case at the subsequent trial, was that when van Wyk and Moller had excavated the hole to a reasonable depth, van Wyk struck the young man on the head with the shovel or pick and he toppled in head-first, snapping off his trouser buttons as he fell. The assailant then delivered the blow to the back with the pick to see if Moller really was dead. Finding that he was, he refilled the hole and threw the shovel and pick away. The implements found on the Beamish farm were subsequently identified as the ones Moller had borrowed from the park in Bloemfontein.

The police did not have to look very far for van Wyk. On Friday afternoon he saw a report of the case in the Johannesburg *Star* saying that the police were looking for both Moller and van Wyk. He returned to Bloemfontein by train on Saturday and gave himself up at the CID headquarters on Sunday morning.

The trial of van Wyk opened at the Supreme Court in Bloemfontein on 21 October 1930 before the judge-president, Sir Etienne de Villiers. He was prosecuted by the attorney-general, Mr W.F. Hoal, while Mr F.P. de Wet appeared for the defence.

Van Wyk had told a brother-in-law, who came to visit him in prison, that he felt he'd been double-crossed by a member of the family, though he didn't say who it was. He gave the impression that the man had betrayed him to the police, stolen his money and given his wife and family the minimum of help. And he had hinted that he would deal with this relative when he came out of prison.

Van Wyk was the last person known to have been with the young man, had been seen after the death of Moller near to where the body was found and was known to have been driving his car without the key, which was afterwards discovered in Moller's pocket.

The plaster casts of the footprints found near where the shovel had been discovered, proved to be very similar in size and shape to van Wyk's own boots. And mud deposits taken from his boots were shown to be identical to the mud from the side of the pool.

When the defence began its case, van Wyk went into the witness-box and made a long statement. Having described going with Moller to look for buried money at Waterval, he continued:

It was fully dark when we got to the vicinity of the hole. I remembered, more or less, the place where the money had been buried, but when we got there we saw that there were two holes and each had been refilled to about eighteen inches from the top.

We decided to open both holes and started on one, digging alternately, until we reached the bottom. Then I got into the hole and took the pick to see if I could use it to lift the stone which was covering the money. Takkie asked me where the nearest place was to get some water, and I pointed out the windmill. As far as I remember he was squatting down at the top of the hole, looking towards the windmill, and I was in the hole.

I lifted the pick and swung it back, preparing to strike the ground, when I heard Takkie yell. I guessed that the point of the pick must have struck him in the back. I turned round and saw that he was overbalancing and falling backwards. I dropped the pick and tried to grab him, but he crashed against me, knocking me against the side of the hole. Then he seemed to go head first into the hole. I heard a thud and felt him go still. I stooped and felt for him. He was limp and the pick was underneath him and I guessed that he had caught his head on the pick as he fell into the bottom of the hole. I tried to revive him with water from the windmill, but it was useless. I realized that he was dead.

Then I seemed to have a black-out. When I came to myself again, I was near the car. My feet were bare and sore and my whole body was exhausted, but I still had my boots with me.

This story was backed up by Dr J.H. Lawlor, a medical practitioner from Bloemfontein. He had actually gone to Waterval and stood in the jackal hole. With an assistant squatting on the lip of the pit, looking in the direction of the windmill, he had been able to show that it was perfectly possible for a man, swinging a pick in the hole, to catch the other man in the back. And he had photographs taken to prove the point. The doctor pointed out that the fracture of the skull was also compatible with a man falling and striking his head on a pick already in the bottom of the pit.

Van Wyk made a good impression in court. The tall serious figure in the witness-box told his story in a calm and convincing manner. Cross-examined as to why he had not told anyone about the accident, he simply explained that he was torn between making a clean breast of everything, taking his own life, or running away. And in the end he had just run away.

The defence also asked the question: Would a man of strong religious convictions such as van Wyk really lure a relative to a remote spot and carefully plan his murder, merely because he thought the young man had stolen some money from him?

The jury agreed with the defence and on Saturday afternoon, 25 October 1930, brought in a verdict of not guilty. There was a roar of applause in the courtroom, and another spontaneous burst of cheering greeted the announcemnent that the verdict had been unanimous. People surged around him, as he stood tall in the dock, trying to shake him by the hand, and the police had difficulty keeping them at bay and clearing a way for him as he walked, a free man, from the court.

The only note of discord was provided by Mrs Moller. As she made her way out of court she passed the pile of clothes belonging to her late son, exhibits in the case, displayed on a table. She stretched out her hand as if to touch them, and sobs shook her slight frame as she cried: 'O my son, my son!'

Van Wyk could not find work. He had no money to set himself up in business and applications for assistance in finding jobs to the magistrates' office and the Provincial Administration authorities in Bloemfontein were unsuccessful. It was a time of depression and unemployment in South Africa.

He moved north to Johannesburg, but was no more successful there. January 1931 found him near Carolina, a coal-mining area some 150 miles east of Johannesburg. But van Wyk was looking for agricultural work.

After trudging from farm to farm for several days he stopped one hot day at a road-mender's hut to ask for some refreshment. The man gladly gave van Wyk a drink and they got into conversation.

'I don't think you'll find any farm work around here,' said the man. 'The nearest one is Tucker's and I know for a fact that he's thinking of selling up.'

'Business is that bad?'

The man nodded his head. 'He's an Englishman. Getting on a bit, I suppose, and wants to get back to the old country. His wife's already gone back, I believe, and he's got no family living with him.'

Van Wyk nodded his head in turn. 'Not much point going there then.'

He thanked the man for the drink and set off on the road again.

Cyril Grigg Tucker was fifty-seven years old and only five foot 4 inches tall. He'd been living on the farm, Appeldorn, being looked after by black South African servants, since his wife had gone back to England for a holiday at the end of the previous year.

His neighbour and great friend, Henry Stewart, had a farm some four miles away and grazed some of his cattle and sheep on Tucker's land. The agreement was that they would share the profits when the animals were sold.

Stewart called to see Tucker on 29 January and was introduced to the tall figure of van Wyk.

'Mr van Wyk is staying with me for a few days, Henry. He's thinking of buying the farm and the stock. Yours too if you like.'

As prices were then low for sheep and cattle, Henry Stewart was not averse to selling some of his, if he could get a good price for them. They haggled a bit and finally settled on £1,021. It was to be a cash sale.

'Mr van Wyk and I will fix up the deal in Pretoria,' announced Tucker. 'We'll be going there in a few days to see our solicitors.' Privately, he told Stewart that the tall man had offered £3,500 for his farm and stock.

But Stewart counselled caution. 'Do take care, Cyril, you don't know anything about this chap.'

'What can go wrong, Henry? I'm not signing anything until I'm sure he has the money.'

On 3 February, still the hot, but rainy, season in South Africa, some more neighbours called: John and Enid Fleming, who owned the farm next to Stewart's. They arrived in the afternoon and, after being introduced to van Wyk, they all had tea together on the veranda.

Tucker was in the best of spirits. 'We're off to Pretoria tomorrow,' he announced cheerfully, 'to finally fix up the sale of the farm.'

The Flemings invited Tucker and van Wyk to dine with them that evening and together the two men drove to the Fleming farm. It was dark when they returned at ten-thirty. Thunder was rolling about the dark sky, which was occasionally lit by flashes of lightning, and it was just beginning to rain.

A week later Stewart was in the small town of Carolina

for the market. He saw the head of a tall man sticking up above the crowd at a cattle auction and recognized van Wyk. He pushed through the crowd to him.

'How's Cyril Tucker?'

'Still in Pretoria, as far as I know,' said van Wyk carelessly. 'We went there by car about a week ago and I came back by train. I'm staying at a hotel here in town.'

Some time later Stewart was walking along one of the streets in Carolina when he saw an ox-cart in the road and nearby a pen with some cows in it. He stopped because he recognized the cart as one he had left on Tucker's farm. And as he looked more closely at the cows he recognized that they belonged to him as well.

He went in search of van Wyk and found him looking over a sheep pen.

He strode up to the tall man and seized him by the arm. 'Look here, I object very strongly to the removal of my property. That ox-cart and the cows belong to me. And – My God! They're my sheep as well! What do you mean by taking them off the farm without telling me?'

Van Wyk looked down at the flushed face of the farmer. 'They're mine. I've bought them from Tucker.'

'You haven't bought them from me. I've had no money for them, nor any documentation of the sale. If you've bought them from Tucker, where's the receipt?'

Van Wyk fumbled in the inside pocket of his jacket and brought out a paper. He handed it to Stewart, who looked through it hurriedly.

'That's not a receipt! That's simply a list of goods. It's not even signed by Tucker.'

'He didn't give me a receipt.'

Stewart's jaw dropped as he looked in disbelief at the big man. But he could only stand and stare as van Wyk hurried off.

Stewart, however, wasn't going to let things rest there. He went to the police station and explained his suspicions that van Wyk had cheated both himself and Tucker, if nothing worse.

Van Wyk was duly interviewed and a search of his room
at the hotel in Carolina revealed a basket containing cups
and other silverware, some of it engraved with the name
Cyril Tucker.

The police then questioned Tucker's servants and farm
employees.

The houseboy reported that he had seen van Wyk arrive
at the farm one rainy night and had been given a bed in the
spare room. The last time he'd seen Tucker had been the
night he and van Wyk went to dinner with the Flemings.
The next morning he took Tucker a cup of tea, but the
farmer was not in his room and his bed hadn't been slept in.
He took tea into van Wyk's room and found him fully
dressed. The tall man reported that he had left Tucker in
Carolina.

After breakfast, van Wyk told the houseboy that they had
to pack up Tucker's things as the farmer was going to
Pretoria and would pick up the articles in Carolina. They
filled box after box with the farmer's possessions and
placed them in Tucker's car. Van Wyk then drove it off.
Later he returned and said that the farm now belonged to
him. 'We believed him,' said the man. 'He is a white man
and we are only natives.'

Soon after that van Wyk ordered an old irrigation ditch to
be filled in, but the labourers who worked on it said that it
had been empty before they recharged it with dirt.

A wide search was instituted for Tucker. Enquiries were
made all over the Carolina region and as far away as Pretoria
and Johannesburg, but no trace of him was found. A careful
search of the Tucker farm, however, revealed a
bloodstained box and a similarly stained hammer. The
police went back to the filled-in ditch and reopened it.
When they had dug up about a third they came across Tucker's body. The bluff of van Wyk's, having the ditch filled in
so that the workmen could later say it was empty, and then
burying the body there afterwards, had been called.

Tucker had been beaten about the head and his skull shattered.

Van Wyk was charged with his murder.

This time the circumstantial evidence against him was overwhelming. He had been seen trying to sell Tucker's valuables and even some of his clothes, not to mention the stock on the farm. He was the last person known to have been with Tucker and the motive, this time, was perfectly clear: the acquisiton of a farm worth £3,500.

Van Wyk again admitted the killing, but this time his story was pitiably thin. He said that Tucker had asked him to sleep in the same bedroom with him after the dinner, then made an improper suggestion. A fight broke out and van Wyk, thinking Tucker was going to get a gun to shoot him, clubbed him down with a metal doorstop.

This doorstop was never discovered. The servants remembered no such object, and, in fact, forensic evidence showed the murder weapon to have been a hammer.

Defence counsel pleaded insanity. But the jury would have none of this and a verdict of premeditated murder was brought in.

The judge-president, Mr Justice D. de Waal, sentenced van Wyk to death and he was hanged on 12 June 1931.

7   Robert Clements:
Dosing with Death

It was 11.15 at night when the telephone began ringing. Dr Andrew Brown roused himself slowly from his slumbers and put out a sleepy hand to the bedside table.

'You'd think patients would leave you alone at the Bank Holiday,' he muttered as his scrabbling hand found the telephone and lifted the receiver. His wife in the bed beside him made only some incoherent noise and put her head under the blankets.

'It's Dr Clements here,' came a high piping voice at the other end of the telephone. 'It's my wife. I think she's dying. Can you come at once?'

After replying, Dr Brown put down the receiver and leaned back against the headboard. That's all I need, he thought – the perfect end to a pleasant day on the sands at Southport!

It was Whitsun Bank Holiday, 26 May 1947.

Dr Brown's wife now roused herself and lifted a sleepy face to him. 'Who was that, Andrew?'

'It was that nuisance Dr Clements and his wife.'

'Are you going?'

'I shall have to, shan't I?' he said somewhat irritably. 'The last time I saw her – and that's only two or three days ago – she was as right as rain. But now he says she's dying.'

'Still, if it's Dr Clements ...'

'Oh yes, I know. The eminent Dr Clements, pillar of Southport society and all that. Well, he may have been a brilliant doctor at one time, but now he's getting past it.'

'What's the matter with his wife?' asked Mrs Brown hurriedly.

Her husband leaned back in bed, showing no inclination to get up. 'That's it. I don't really know. He's had Dr Holmes to see her, and he diagnosed a brain tumour. I didn't believe it myself and told Clements he ought to send her to a proper brain specialist if they suspected that. But I examined her anyway, as he asked me to, and all I could find were signs of slight toxaemia. I took a blood sample, but all it showed was minor iron deficiency.'

'Don't you think you ought to be going?'

'I am,' said Dr Brown, getting out of bed. But he continued to talk as he moved round the room putting on his clothes. 'I think I told you that I called several times to deliver the report, but each time they weren't at home and in the end I pushed it through the letter-box. I also went round after that, but nobody answered the door – they don't even have a servant you see – and the phone seemed to be cut off at the time.'

'Yes, I remember you telling me that.'

'Then he rang me again and said: would I call? I tell you, I didn't want the case. There's nothing worse than doctors' relatives as patients. She's not on my list anyway. She's Holmes's patient. But he pleaded with me to go round and in the end I did. Have I got a clean shirt?'

'In the top drawer of the dressing-table. Well, what happened then?'

'He had this silly idea that his wife was having epileptic attacks in her sleep, without her knowing about it, caused by pressure on the brain from a tumour. Of course, I again told him he ought to have her examined by a brain surgeon. But he said she wouldn't have any more doctors looking at her and flatly refused to go into hospital or a nursing home. Haven't I any more socks?'

'Bottom of the chest of drawers.'

'Thanks. When I finally saw her she said she felt better than she had for a long time. Mind you, I've never seen her on her own. Clements is always hanging about in the room. My own opinion is that she's not being looked after properly. The flat is an absolute disgrace, untidy and rubbish all over the place. Anyway, all that was only a couple of days ago. And now he says she's dying! Well, I suppose I'd better go.'

He kissed his wife and left.

When Dr Brown arrived at 20, the Promenade, the imposing three-storeyed block of flats on the front at Southport, where Dr and Mrs Clements lived, he found that his ideas, as to the seriousness of the case, needed revising.

As usual he had to hold his nose as he entered the flat. The smell of rotting food from the kitchen and the squalor of the apartment were more appropriate for a rubbish tip than for the living quarters of one of the richest couples in town. He found Mrs Clements lying on a bed without sheets and whose blankets needed a good wash.

She was unconscious and her respirations alternated between deep gasping breaths and periods when she hardly seemed to be breathing at all. He took her pulse and listened to her heart.

'Your wife looks to be quite ill, Dr Clements.'

'I must get some help then.' He was a short dumpy-looking man with a bald head and was standing at the end of the bed, jerking from one foot to the other. 'Do you mind if I get hold of my wife's best friend?'

'I think that would be an excellent idea. And while you're away I'll give your wife a thorough examination.'

Several times during the examination her breathing slowed down and a faint blue coloration appeared in her lips and cheeks, but then she seemed to recover. He raised her eyelids and noted that her pupils were small.

When Dr Clements returned with a middle-aged lady he introduced as Mrs Stevens, Dr Brown said. 'I'm very worried about your wife, Dr Clements, we shall have to get her into hospital.'

'Nursing home,' said the doctor. 'She wouldn't like it in hospital. I'll ring the Astley Bank Nursing Home.'

'Better ring for an ambulance – and get in touch with Dr Holmes.'

When the ambulance arrived for Mrs Clements, Dr Brown drove Mrs Stevens and Dr Clements to the nursing home in his car. And when Dr Holmes arrived later the three doctors discussed the case round Mrs Clements's bed, while the matron, Mrs Baxendale, stood in the background with one of her nurses.

Dr Holmes examined her eyes with an ophthalmoscope. He stood up and shook his head. 'What do you think, Doctor?' he said, handing the instrument to Dr Brown.

Dr Brown took the instrument and tried to use it, but soon handed it back. 'The pupils are really too small to be examined,' he said.

Dr Holmes nodded his head, but this time he addressed her husband. 'I think a quarter of a grain of morphine to try and calm the breathing?'

But Dr Brown hurriedly retorted, 'Oh, I think that's far too much! A sixth, or an eighth of a grain, or even less. In fact, I'm not happy about her having morphine at all.'

'Perhaps you're right,' said Dr Holmes.

Having got the patient into a nursing home Dr Brown now felt that he had done all he reasonably could, and thoughts of the warm bed he had left several hours before began to return to his mind. After all, Mrs Clements was Dr Holmes's patient, not his. He bade the others good-night. But as he was leaving the room the matron caught his eye and gave him a long and significant look.

She caught him up as he walked down the silent corridor.

'What do you think about her?' she asked him, her face expressionless and looking straight ahead.

Dr Brown looked sideways at her. 'What do you,' he returned.

Mrs Baxendale halted in her tracks and looked back over her shoulder. 'Do you want me to speak frankly, Doctor?' she replied.

Dr Brown stopped too and together they stood facing each other in the middle of the deserted corridor. 'Certainly, Matron.'

'Well, it looks to me more like an overdose of morphia than cerebral trouble.'

Dr Brown was silent for some time. Then he said quietly, 'I agree that the Cheyne-Stokes respiration and the pin-point pupils are an indication of morphine poisoning, but there are several other possible causes for the coma she's in. However, it might be as well to make sure that she doesn't receive any narcotics.'

'I'll do what I can, Doctor.'

'She's not my patient, she's Dr Holmes's – and I don't really want to interfere. But I'd be obliged if you'd keep me informed as to her progress.'

The matron said that she would and the doctor departed.

In Mrs Clements's room her husband and Dr Holmes were talking.

'We had a meal out during the early part of the evening,' reported Dr Clements. 'Then we went for a walk. She seemed quite all right. As you know, she's been a lot better lately. Well, all of a sudden, she collapsed. I had difficulty getting her back to the flat. Then, when we got in, she went into a coma. I tried to ring you, but you weren't at home.'

'One of those interminable dinners,' said Dr Holmes. 'You then phoned Dr Brown?'

'I had to. I had to do something.'

'Quite right. You did the right thing.'

Dr Holmes eventually went back home.

At about nine o'clock the next morning Mrs Baxendale

rang him to say that his patient had just died. The doctor expressed his sorrow then asked to speak to Dr Clements.

'I'm sorry to intrude into your grief like this, Dr Clements, but I need your permission for a post-mortem.'

'Whatever do you want to do that for?' returned the reedy voice at the other end of the telephone.

'Because I'm not absolutely certain of the cause of death.'

Dr Clements's high voice was so accentuated by the phone that it became almost a squeak. 'But you told me she had a brain tumour!'

'I said,' came the calm voice of Dr Holmes, 'that I had a strong suspicion of a cerebral tumour. But you as a doctor will appreciate that I want to see the nature and the situation of it, if it is present.'

'I'm afraid that I cannot allow you to indulge yourself in this way,' squeaked Clements. 'My wife would not have wanted her body interfered with like that. I know you will think this is illogical, but I feel I must respect her wishes in this matter.'

'I can fully appreciate how you feel, of course,' put in Dr Holmes quickly, 'but I must point out that it would be difficult for me to sign a death certificate without knowing the precise cause of death. And I couldn't be sure of that without an autopsy.'

Dr Holmes could hear a drumming sound at the other end of the telephone, which he assumed must be Dr Clements's fingers tapping on the receiver. Eventually Dr Clements voice came through.

'Very well. If you are going to resort to blackmail, I have no alternative but to comply.' And he slammed down the receiver.

But Dr Holmes had no intention of conducting the post-mortem himself. He was chairman of the medical board at the Southport Infirmary and he immediately phoned the pathologist there, Dr James Montague Houston, and asked him to come over to the nursing home and perform the autopsy.

Dr Houston agreed and later that day they met at the nursing home. After an external examination of the body, they studied the brain and discovered a little extra fluid lying on and between its membranes. However, there was no other abnormality and no sign of a brain tumour. This came as rather a shock to Dr Holmes. He asked his colleague to carry on with the rest of the examination.

The pathologist drew his attention to the evidence of anaemia in the tissues. The stomach was also distended with a large quantity of liquid.

'Since we haven't yet found the cause of death,' remarked Dr Holmes, 'I expect you will be analysing the stomach contents, won't you?'

'Certainly,' replied Dr Houston. 'I'll also be taking some blood samples.'

'You'll be removing some of the organs?'

'Yes, I'll take them back to the lab, for further examination tomorrow.'

It was 11.30 at night when Dr Holmes left the pathologist to continue the post-mortem.

The next day he rang him at the pathological laboratory.

'The cause of death, in my opinion,' said Dr Houston, 'was myeloid leukaemia.'

'Really?' said Dr Holmes in surprise. 'I certainly didn't suspect that.'

'I prepared microscope slides from the blood samples I took,' continued Dr Houston, rather defensively, 'and from an examination of these I noted an increase in the polymorphonuclear cells.'

'I didn't notice any enlargement of the spleen,' argued Dr Holmes. 'Isn't that usual in these cases?'

'I thought there was a slight enlargement. And I showed the microscope slides to Dr Cronin Lowe and he agreed with me that it looked like myeloid leukaemia.'

'Well, you're the expert, and I must admit that the disease does have some very peculiar symptoms.'

'There was also the evidence of anaemia in the tissues.'

'Oh yes, I don't doubt it. Will you sign the death certificate, giving that as the cause of death?' The pathologist agreed. Later that day Dr Clements called at Dr Holmes's surgery for the death certificate for his late wife. He then arranged for the funeral to be held on Friday.

But on the same day the death certificate was signed, someone called at the main police station in Southport and made a statement about the death of Mrs Clements. This person was never afterwards identified by the police or the coroner and did not appear as a witness at the subsequent inquest. But as a result the deputy chief constable of Southport, Detective Superintendent W.H. Lloyd, took the statement to his superior, Lieutenant Colonel Harold Mighall, the chief constable, and laid it on his desk.

Colonel Mighall read the report through carefully. Then he tapped it with his finger. 'Have you done anything about this yet?'

'Yes sir. I've informed the coroner, Mr Cornelius Bolton, and he's going to call in the Home Office pathologist and have another post-mortem done.'

'Good.' The chief constable leaned back in his chair. 'Take a seat, Superintendent, and tell me what you think.'

'Well sir,' said the detective, sitting in the chair by the desk. 'If it is morphia-poisoning, then it could be suicide, accidental death, or even homicide.'

Colonel Mighall nodded his head. 'I may be able to help you with that, but first let me ask you what you know about this Dr Clements?'

The superintendent ran a hand through his hair. 'I looked him up before I came up to your office, of course. He's sixty-seven years old – semi-retired now. Up to last September he was deputy medical officer of health for Blackburn.'

'Correct. Did you also know that he is a leader of the Southport branch of the Friends of Czechoslovakia, a

member of the Southport Psychology Society and the Park
Ward Conservative Association, as well as having once
been a prominent Freemason?'

The detective's eyes opened wide. 'You seem to know a
lot about him.'

The chief constable nodded his head again. 'I do. I know
a very great deal about Dr Clements. Did you know, for
example, that the late Mrs Clements was his fourth wife?'

'Let me see if I can guess, sir – she was an heiress?'

'Good guess. Her father left her £22,000.'

The superintendent whistled, and the chief constable
continued.

'Let me tell you a little about the good Dr Clements. This
was before your time, of course, but in 1928 Clements
married for the third time. A Katherine Burke, I think she
was. They were wed in Manchester, but moved up to
Southport, and in 1939 she died of cancer. At least that's
what it said on the death certificate, but then that was
made out by Dr Clements himself.'

'Nothing illegal about that, sir,' put in the detective.

'True,' said the chief constable, 'but wait a minute. A
friend of hers, in fact it was her doctor, Dr Irene Gayus,
came to me and said she thought the death was
suspicious. The third Mrs Clements had always been
robust and active and her decline had been very rapid –
too rapid, according to the doctor. I thought there were
sufficient grounds for having an autopsy. But Dr Gayus
was just too late coming to me. When I phoned, the body
was already in the crematorium and there was no way of
stopping the service proceeding.'

'Did you find out anything about Dr Clements? Did he
have a girlfriend or anything like that?'

The chief constable shook his head. We couldn't find
one. He was certainly a bit of a lady's man and he lived
well, but that was all. But taken together with the recent
suspicious death, it's all a bit too much of a coincidence.'
He leaned across the table towards the superintendent. 'I

want this thing running down exhaustively.' He waggled his finger at the detective. 'I don't want Clements to get away with it a second time!'

The police interviewed Joseph Milward and his wife, who had been very friendly with the Clementses for the past four years. According to Milward, Mrs Clements had told him she'd had a bad turn the previous November. She had been out with her husband in the car, while he visited patients, when she suddenly had an attack during which she seemed to lose the use of her limbs. Dr Clements had to drive her home and, after getting her up the stairs with great difficulty, managed to relieve the paralysis by massaging her legs.

The following month Dr Clements visited the Milwards and told them that his wife was ill in bed with jaundice and that he had called in Dr Holmes. When they finally saw her again, in March, she had lost a lot of weight and her face was still yellow. Nevertheless, when she appeared at their house on 24 May, only a few days before she died, she seemed quite well.

Meanwhile, a post-mortem was conducted on Mrs Clements by Dr W.H. Grace, the Home Office pathologist, and some organs sent to Dr J.B. Firth, the director of the Home Office Forensic Science laboratory in Preston, for analysis. He had a difficult job, for the organs removed and examined by Dr Houston after the first post-mortem had been destroyed by him after his analyses were complete. But, in what was later described as a breakthrough in forensic science, Dr Firth and his colleagues discovered traces of morphine in parts of the spinal cord and the overall conclusion of the autopsy was that Mrs Clements had died from morphine poisoning.

At the subsequent inquest Dr Grace reported that morphine tablets would dissolve in warm water. The solution could be injected by a hypodermic syringe. If a lethal dose were taken the effects would take about half to three-quarters of an hour to appear. There would be mental confusion on the part of the subject. Their limbs would become weak, and they would gradually sink into unconsciousness.

The police began a tour of the chemists' shops in Southport, during which Detective Sergeant John Thompson went into the premises of James Righton Ltd, in Lord Street, and explained to the manager that he wanted to trace drug sales to a Dr Clements.

The manager asked the detective back to his office and produced the relevant books.

'Here's an entry,' said he man. 'January 11th: twenty-five half-grain morphine sulphate tablets on a prescription made out to himself, Dr Clements, for use in his practice. Is that the sort of thing you're looking for?'

'That's exactly the thing I'm looking for.'

'Here's another. January 20th: twenty half-grain morphine sulphate, again made out to Dr Clements, and another for the same amount on March 20th.'

Sergeant Thompson made a careful note of these. Then he closed his notebook with a snap and climbed to his feet. 'Thank you very much, you've been most helpful.' He was about to leave when the manager, who had been running his eye down the columns in the ledger, stopped him.

'Wait a minute. Here's something else. Another two entries, one for February 13th and one for April 3rd, both for twenty-five half-grain morphine sulphate tablets, both signed by Dr Clements, but not for him. They were for a Mrs Proctor.'

'And did he actually collect these prescriptions himself?'

'I can soon find out by checking with my assistants.' He went out of the office carrying the open book in his arms. A short while later he returned. 'He collected at least one of these prescriptions made out to Mrs Proctor, because my assistant knows Dr Clements well and recognized him when he came in.'

Sergeant Thompson obtained Mrs Proctor's address from the pharmacist and immediately went to the house in Mornington Road. The front door was answered by a middle-aged lady who looked at him suspiciously.

The detective produced his warrant card and introduced himself. 'Are you Mrs Proctor?' he asked.

'No, I am not. I'm Mrs Proctor's companion, Mrs Rogerson,' she said severely.

'I'd very much like a word with Mrs Proctor.'

'Young man, Mrs Proctor is eighty-five years old, largely bedridden, and she doesn't receive visitors.'

Sergeant Thompson looked down at the solid figure of Mrs Rogerson planted immovably in the doorway and sighed. 'All I want to do, Mrs Rogerson, is to consult her about the medication she's been receiving from Dr Clements.'

'I can tell you all you need to know about that.' There was a pause, as if Mrs Rogerson was making up her mind. Then she beckoned him inside.

She led him into a drawing-room with heavy old-fashioned furniture and bade him sit in an overstuffed armchair while she sat primly opposite.

'How often did Dr Clements call to see Mrs Proctor?' asked the detective, taking out his notebook.

'Once a week. I always showed him in here, and he sat where you are now. I always gave him a progress report on Mrs Proctor before I showed him up to her room. Then I would take him up and remain while he examined her. She said this with a faintly disapproving air as if she felt that Dr Clements could not be trusted to examine the old lady alone.

'And what kind of medication did Dr Clements prescribe?' His pen was poised above the page of his notebook.

'Soneryl tablets.'

'I beg your pardon?'

'Soneryl tablets,' repeated the lady with rather more than a trace of impatience in her voice. 'They are always in a box, which I collected from the chemist. Mrs Proctor takes two each night.'

'You collected them?'

'I said so, didn't I?' Plainly Mrs Rogeron was becoming annoyed at having to repeat everything twice.

The detective pursed his lips. 'And did the doctor ever inject Mrs Proctor? Or give her anything himself?'

'Certainly not!'

The sergeant made his way back to the station in a thoughtful mood.

On Thursday evening Dr Clements took a party to dinner at the Stella Maris restaurant not far from his flat. There was Mr and Mrs Milward, Dr Clements's 22-year-old son George, who had recently been demobilized from the Navy and had come over from Belfast for the funeral of his stepmother, and Dr Clements's brother Ernest.

After dinner the Milwards accompanied the doctor back to his flat. Soon after they arrived there came a knock at the front door and Dr Clements went to answer it. He came back in a few minutes with a puzzled look on his face.

'That's funny,' he said. 'That was the lady from the downstairs flat. She said the police called some time ago wanting to speak to me and asked if I would ring them. I'd better do that straight away, if you'll excuse me?'

He went away again and was back a short time later.

'That's very strange. The police want me to go to the mortuary and identify my wife's body.'

A few minutes later a police car pulled up outside the house and Dr Clements was driven off.

This was the first occasion the Milwards had been alone in the flat and they used the time Dr Clements was away to try and clean it up a little. They finished with eleven sacks of rubbish, but even that hardly seemed to make much difference.

When Dr Clements returned he was looking rather worried. But he put a brave face on it. 'There's going to be an inquest tomorrow at ten o'clock and I shall have to attend. But it will only take about five minutes. Simply a matter of identification. Then we can go ahead with the funeral as arranged.'

A few minutes later the telephone rang and Dr Clements went into the other room to answer it. When he came back his face was looking strained.

'What do you think, Joe? The police talk as if there is something fishy about my wife's death.'

'Don't worry about it, Bertie. You'll soon be able to straighten them out on that.'

'I hope so.'

'Of course you will. Now I think we'd better get off. Leave you in peace.'

'You'll be able to come round tomorrow morning? To help me with the people who're coming for the funeral? Mr Dennison, the funeral director, will be coming, of course. But I'd like some moral support.'

'We'll be there, Bertie, never fear. About 10.30.'

Later that same night a conference was held in the chief constable's office. Sergeant Thompson made his report.

'I've checked up on Soneryl tablets. They're barbiturate-based sleeping tablets. No morphine in them at all.'

'So what we've established then,' remarked Superintendent Lloyd, 'is that Clements purchased considerable quantities of morphia in the form of morphine sulphate tablets, some at least for a patient who wasn't taking it. I think we've grounds for an arrest on that alone.'

The chief constable assented. 'We'll get a warrant tomorrow for his arrest. And we must get the funeral stopped tomorrow before it goes ahead.'

At about 9.30 the next morning, Mr J.H. Dennison informed the vicar of Christ Church that the funeral would not be going ahead that day. He next went to call on Dr Clements, whom he found unshaven and still in his pyjamas.

'I'm sorry to have to tell you, Dr Clements, that the funeral has been cancelled.'

'The devil it has! Why is that?'

'I'm sorry, I don't know. The policeman didn't give me a reason, but he had written authority from the coroner to stop the funeral.'

Dr Clements made no reply. He appeared to be rather dazed. Then he wandered off into another room. Mr Dennison stood looking after him. Often bereaved people behaved somewhat oddly and it was normally best just to await developments. So he sat down. But Clements didn't reappear.

After waiting some time he stood up again. 'Dr Clements! Are you there?'

There was only silence in the untidy flat.

Dennison went to the door of the sitting-room. 'Dr Clements!'

Still there was no reply. He was now getting worried and went through the door into the rest of the flat. Eventually he found a bedroom. And in it, on top of the bed, lay Dr Clements.

Dennison tried to rouse him, but couldn't. The doctor was deeply unconscious. Then the undertaker noticed a hypodermic syringe in a bowl on the bedside table and a piece of paper with a hurried scrawl in pencil upon it.

> My dear Ernie and George – I cannot stand this diabolical insult to me … Please, Ernie and George, carry on. God bless you. Always – Bertie.

Dr Clements died soon after being admitted to hospital.

On the following Monday morning Dr Houston was found slumped in his chair in the pathological laboratory of Southport Infirmary. He had poisoned himself with cyanide. On his desk was a note which said in part:

> I have for some time been aware that I have been making mistakes. I have not profited from experience. I was convinced that Mrs Clements died of leukaemia, and accordingly destroyed the vital organs after completing my autopsy.

His death, along with those of Clements's wives, is one of the tragic features of the case. A diabetic, and probably not a stable one (since his colleagues noted that he often smelled of acetone, indicating high blood-sugar level), he was undoubtedly unwell when he conducted the post-mortem on Mrs Clements. Moreover, he was probably influenced by Dr Holmes into thinking there was nothing suspicious about her death.

The inquest jury came to the conclusion that he took his own life, but the balance of his mind was so disturbed that he didn't know what he was doing.

They came to a rather harsher conclusion about the other two deaths, deciding that Amy Victoria Clements was murdered by her husband, Dr Robert George Clements and that the doctor committed *felo de se* – literally 'self murder.'

8 Ernest Dyer:
Partner in Crime

'Just a minute. I'd like a word with you.' Detective Inspector Abbot of the Scarborough Constabulary approached the short man standing on the edge of the pavement.

It was a cold day in November and the wind from the sea roared up Bar Street, making their coats flap around their legs.

'What do you want?' asked the man. He was wearing one of those large grey hats which were the feature of the man-about-town in the 1920s. But he was having to hold on to it in the blustery wind.

Detective Abbot reached into his pocket for his notebook. 'Is your name Fitzsimmons?'

'Yes it is. What's it got to do with you?'

'I'm a police officer.' The inspector showed his warrant card. 'Is there somewhere we can talk?'

The man hesitated then nodded his head. He pointed to the hotel just behind him, which was called the Old Bar Hotel. 'I'm staying there. We can go inside.'

He led the way through the front door into a hall and then into a room on the left. It was a small lounge with a coal fire burning brightly in the grate on the furthest wall, and it was empty.

Fitzsimmons took up a position with his back to the fire.

'Won't you sit down, Inspector?'

Abbot shook his head. He flipped the pages of his notebook. 'Will you tell me your full name?'

'What's this all about, Inspector?'

'I'd like your full name, sir. If you don't mind?'

The man sighed. 'James Vincent Fitzsimmons.'

'And your address?'

The man gave an address in Butcher-gate, Carlisle.

'Can you give me any proof of your identity?'

'Look here, Inspector, this is ridiculous. My father's a well-known JP in Carlisle. He can vouch for me. And I should like to know why I'm being asked to account for myself like this. Is it because of the advert I put in the local paper?'

It was indeed because of the advertisement Fitzsimmons had put in the *Scarborough Evening News* and *Daily Post*. It had read:

> Wanted a few gentlemen of highest integrity as agents; no capital required. Apply Fitzsimmons, Old Bar Hotel.

Since this was 1922 there were quite a number of ex-servicemen about, who, though unemployed, still had gratuities from their war service. Several of these had been interviewed by Fitzsimmons. But, contrary to what he had indicated in the advertisement, he had seemed interested less in giving the men jobs as agents than in trying to get them to invest in get-rich-quick schemes. And some had complained to the police that they thought Fitzsimmons was a con man.

The inspector had discovered that a certain Fitzsimmons had also been passing dud cheques in various hotels in the North.

'How long have you been here?' asked Abbot.

'What's today, Thursday? I came on Saturday.'

'And where were you before that?'

'Let me see now,' said Fitzsimmons calmly, 'I left home eight days ago and went to Manchester, but didn't stay there. I'm travelling in connection with my father's business, you see. He's a wholesale and retail tailor and we are going to open an agency here selling velour hats.'

'What's your home phone number?' asked Abbot.

'What?' For the first time in their conversation Fitzsimmons's calm exterior seemed to crack. He looked worried. 'We're not on the phone. My father, you see. He's a bit old-fashioned. Doesn't like phones.'

'Well, what about the business phone? You must be on the phone for business. What's the number for that?'

'I, er … can't remember it.'

Detective Inspector Abbot allowed a silence to develop between them. 'I tell you what, sir,' said the inspector eventually. 'We'll go down to the station while you think about it. There I'll be able to get in touch with your father for sure and it'll save me having to rush backwards and forwards from there to here to talk to you.'

At that moment Detective Constable Nalton entered the room.

'Ah Nalton, Mr Fitzsimmons is coming to the station wih us. Pop along and see the proprietress of the hotel and ask her to go upstairs and pack the gentleman's bag for him.'

'That won't be necessary, Inspector. I'll go upstairs and pack the bag myself.'

'Just as you like, sir. My assistant will inform the proprietress that you are leaving. If you'd just like to lead the way, sir.'

For a moment it looked as if Fitzsimmons were going to protest. Then he shrugged his shoulders and marched out of the room.

More than two years before this happened, in July 1920, two young men walked up a leafy lane near Kenley in Surrey. They stopped by a large five-barred gate and looked up at the notice proudly displayed above it: 'The Welcomes Stud Farm'.

Ernest Dyer, the smaller of the two, looked up at his companion. 'Well, what do you think, Eric?'

Eric, whose full name was George Eric Gordon Tombe, chewed his lip. 'Are you sure it's going to work, Bill?' (He always called Ernest Dyer 'Bill'.)

The other slapped his friend on the shoulder. 'Of course it is, Eric. The only people who lose money on horses are the people who bet – people like me,' he finished rather ruefully. 'Everybody else, the bookmakers, the owners, the jockeys, the trainers: they all make a fortune. And that's what we're going to do. We're going to be both owners, because we're going to breed horses, and trainers as well. So we're going to make money both ways. I've engaged a chap to do the hard work, like looking after the horses. All we've got to do is to sit back and rake it in. As you know I have a certain amount of other business interests up and down the country so I won't always be on hand to tell the man what to do. So if you'd pop in occasionally to see that things are all right ...?'

'I'll do that, of course, it's just that since our other ventures didn't turn out so well –'

'It was just the wrong time, Eric. I know that cars are your first love, you being a trained mechanic and all, but there just isn't the money about at the present time for people to buy motors. That was why we failed. Well, I suppose you could say *you* failed, for you put up the money. But I can assure you that this time your money will be as safe as houses. Oh, by the way, I'm going to take out an insurance policy against fire. You just can't be too careful these days. But you don't need to worry about that, Eric, I'll pay the premiums.'

They were two ex-officers who had met after the war when they worked at the Air Ministry. Tombe, who was twenty-eight, had been commissioned in the Royal Artillery and served in France. Dyer, who was a year older, had started his career as a gas-fitter's mate, but had emigrated to Australia when he was seventeen. In 1914 he had joined the Australian Engineers, been wounded at Gallipoli and, after his recovery, had been commissioned in the Royal West Surreys. Later, he transferred as a first lieutenant to the Royal Engineers.

Dyer lived on the stud farm. He, his wife and their two children occupied the large farmhouse called The Welcomes. But he hardly ever seemed to be there. His frequent trips away, however, had a lot less to do with business than with race meetings and gambling on horses. He had given out to everybody, except Eric, that he had won £15,000 by betting the whole of his war gratuity on Furious, the 33-to-1 winner of the 1920 Lincolnshire Handicap, and part of this money had gone to buy the stud farm. But it is far more likely that he lost most of the money he ever had by betting on horses.

As a business venture, the stud farm and training stables were a failure right from the start and it had been going for less than a year when, in April 1921, a mysterious fire destroyed most of the buildings, including the farmhouse and Dyer's furniture.

The insurance company, with whom the place had been heavily covered, was very suspicious and refused to pay up. And Dyer did not pursue the matter. That virtually finished the venture of the racing stables. Tombe, who was equally doubtful about the fire's cause, withdrew from his partnership with Dyer.

Eric Tombe had been living at a hotel in Dorking, Surrey, but he then moved up to London. Still a moderately wealthy young man he engaged a flat at Morris Chambers in London's Haymarket in September 1921. His parents, Revd and Mrs Tombe lived in Sydenham, between Aylesbury and Oxford, at the foot of the Chiltern Hills; but Eric saw little of them. He did, however, have a girlfriend. For the purposes of this story, I'll call her Alice, since, although she did give evidence at the inquest, she was never identified. He had known her since the summer of 1918, used to go and stay at her parents' home in London and had taken her to The Welcomes.

In March 1922, nearly a year after the disastrous fire, Tombe called on Alice in London. She told him that she was going up North for a while and he saw her off from Euston Station. She was due back on 25 April and Eric wrote to tell her that he would meet the train. But when the train drew in it wasn't Tombe she saw waiting beyond the barrier, but Ernest Dyer.

'Hullo! What are you doing here? Where's Eric?'

'I'm afraid I've got bad news for you. Eric has had to go overseas.' Dyer showed her a telegram from Tombe which was addressed to her, and in it he apologized for having to go abroad.

But Alice was an observant girl and knew Eric well. She read the message through again. 'Where's he gone?'

'I think he said he had to go to Paris for a few days.'

'Well then, why doesn't he say so? It simply doesn't sound right to me. Eric doesn't talk like that. I've never heard him say he was going "overseas". It's not one of his expressions.'

Ernest Dyer said nothing. But his face had gone white.

'You know what I think? I think you wrote this yourself, Bill.'

Dyer's voice was dry and scratchy. 'Nothing of the kind.'

But Alice carried on as if he hadn't spoken. 'But why should you do that? Did he ask you to? Has he gone somewhere and doesn't want me to know about it?'

Dyer picked up Alice's case from the platform. His face was no longer quite so pale. 'You're a clever girl, Alice. But I can assure you it's all quite innocent. Eric did rush off in a hurry and he did ask me to send you the telegram. I don't know exactly where he's gone, but it's a business deal he's doing somewhere on the Continent. I'm sure he'll contact you in a few days.'

He began to walk in the direction of the station entrance, still carrying Alice's case, and she followed rather reluctantly. They joined the queue for taxis.

'I'm sorry, Alice, but I really must rush off now.'

'I'm still not happy about this, Bill.'

'I really can't stay any longer.' He took an expensive watch on a chain from the pocket of his waistcoat. 'I'm late for an appointment now.'

But Alice was not so easily put off. 'If I don't get a better explanation from you, Bill, I'll have to make my own enquiries.'

A scared light appeared in the man's eyes again. But it disappeared quickly. 'I promise to contact you in a few days, Alice.'

'Come and see me tonight at my home.'

'I'm afraid I won't be able to manage –'

'Come tonight, Bill, or I'll start asking around myself.'

Dyer said nothing further. And he was still gazing abstractedly into space when Alice got into a taxi and was driven off.

A very reluctant figure appeared at Alice's front door that evening.

'Come in, Bill.' She led him into a sitting-room.

Dyer jumped when he saw two burly young men sitting in armchairs on either side of the fire.

'I hope you don't mind, but I've asked a couple of friends of mine and Eric to be present.'

Dyer made a rapid retreat to the door. 'I'm sorry, Alice. I only called to let you know that I must dash off. Sorry and all that.'

'It's quite all right, Bill, no need to get yourself into a state. They don't mean you any harm.' She took him by the arm. 'They're only here to give me some advice.' She drew him gently back into the room.

'Well, all right then. But I still can't stay very long.'

'In that case, I'll get straight down to business.' Alice had gone to stand in front of the fire with the two beefy young men on either side of her. 'I had a letter from Eric last week, the one where he said he was going to meet me at Euston. But he also mentioned that he was going to visit you at The Welcomes. Did you actually see him?'

'Yes,' gulped Dyer, 'that was the last time I clapped eyes on him. It was Thursday of last week. We'd been talking about getting back into partnership.'

A look of doubt came over Alice's face. 'I thought Eric had broken up your earlier partnership because, well, because he didn't really think you were quite honest.'

Dyer laughed uneasily. 'It was all due to a misunderstanding. But Eric definitely came to see me with a view to getting back together. We had quite a long session together. In fact, it went on so late that he missed the last bus and we had to walk to Croydon to get one. I put him on the bus for London and that's the last I saw of him.'

Dyer, who had come only a little way into the room, stood nervously looking at Alice. She stared back at him for a long time without speaking. Then she said slowly: 'I've been thinking things over and one possible explanation why Eric did not come to meet me is that in some way you've done away with him. I agree that's a bit extreme, but unless you tell me where he is, I'm going to go to Scotland Yard and tell them of my suspicions.'

The words seemed to strike Dyer like physical blows, so that he looked as if he would sink down on the floor. But he pulled himself together. 'If you do that Alice, I might as well blow my brains out. You know that my reputation is so bad, particularly after that business of the fire, that nobody will believe me.' His head sank on to his chest. Then he raised his head and for a moment his eyes glittered. 'All I can do is to betray the confidence of a friend.' He paused then went on slowly. 'He swore me to secrecy, but now I have no alternative but to tell the truth.' He paused again and drew a deep breath. 'Eric has gone off with a girl.'

Alice laughed. 'I don't believe it.'

'It's true. He has been seeing another lady.'

Dyer cowered as one of Alice's brawny friends rose from his chair and approached him in a threatening manner.

'I didn't want to say anything. He swore me to silence,' he gabbled. 'But now I must speak out. The lady has been to his flat in the Haymarket. You can ask the porter there. He's seen them together.'

A look of doubt appeared on Alice's face.

'You don't need to take my word for it,' continued Dyer hurriedly with one eye on the young man now standing near him. 'Ask around. Plenty of people have seen them together.'

'You're making it up, just to get out of telling me what you've done with Eric.'

'I'm not, I'm not! I've met the lady. I'll introduce you to her myself, if that will convince you!'

At last the doubt could be seen taking hold. A look of acute anguish appeared on Alice's face and tears began running down her cheeks.

'I don't want to upset you, but it's perfectly true what I tell you. I don't know where they've gone. But they've gone off together.' He began to edge backwards towards the door and as he reached it flung his final bolt. 'And I do know for a fact – they are engaged.' And with that he fled.

Although Dyer was a practised liar his story about there being another woman in Eric Tombe's life was perfectly true. I'll call her Doris, since she too was never subsequently identified. He had known her for more than a year and had been taking her to dinners and dances. The wonder of it was that Alice had not heard about it before.

Dyer had been introduced to Doris the previous month, but since then he had seen her fairly regularly, mostly at Eric's flat in the Haymarket. In fact he had seen her there with Tombe on the Thursday that the young man had gone to The Welcomes.

Eric had said to Doris: 'Bill and I are thinking of going into business at his place,' which she took to mean The

Welcomes. 'We're going down there this evening. I'll see you tomorrow, if you'd like to come round in the afternoon.'

The next afternoon Doris called at Tombe's flat and, after knocking on the door and getting no reply, let herself in with a key he'd given her. On the mat just inside the front door was a telegram. She picked it up and saw that it was addressed to her. It read: 'SHALL BE AWAY A WEEK, WRITING – ERIC'.

Doris was about to leave when the telephone rang. She lifted the receiver to her ear. A man's voice said: 'Bill speaking, is that you, Eric?'

'No, it's Doris. Eric's not here.'

'Do you know where he is?' said Dyer. 'I'm a bit worried about him, you see. We both had quite a lot to drink last night. I put him on the bus at Croydon at twelve o'clock. I'd just like to be sure he got home all right.'

'He seems to have gone off somewhere, Bill. A telegram was waiting for me when I arrived saying he'd be away a week.'

'I'm going to come round.'

It took some time for Dyer to arrive and when he did, Doris saw that he was still very drunk. His eyes were glazed and his speech was slurred. He began a long tale about how he and Tombe had been together the night before. But as he didn't seem to have anything new to tell her Doris said that she was leaving. Dyer then intimated that he would stay the night in Eric's flat and, since he seemed in no condition to travel far, Doris agreed and said she would look in tomorrow.

When she came back the following afternoon, this time accompanied by a girlfriend, she found Dyer busily packing up Tombe's clothes and putting them in a large trunk of Eric's to which he seemed to have the key.

'What are you doing?' asked Doris.

Dyer's face was white and drawn, which Doris put down to a hangover. And she felt that this may also have

accounted for his manner, which was decidedly brusque.
'Eric asked me to pack up his things and get rid of the flat.'

'Get rid of the flat! Why? Isn't he coming back here?'

'I don't know what he's going to do,' snapped Dyer. 'He
said he'd write to you, didn't he?'

Doris was not made of such stern stuff as Alice and
accepted this meekly. 'I suppose it'll be all right,' she
muttered.

She also noticed that Dyer paid the rent due on the flat
with a cheque taken from Tombe's cheque-book. But
again she said nothing. Dyer, perhaps mollified by the fact
that neither of the girls was prepared to question his
activities, loosened up enough to take both of them out to
dinner. But again he would say no more about Eric's
whereabouts than he had the day before.

Doris never heard anything more from Eric Tombe.

The other people concerned about Eric Tombe's
whereabouts were his parents. Even though they hadn't
been all that close to him and had grown used to seeing
him only a few times a year, they kept in touch by letter,
although it was only through an accommodation address.

Mrs Tombe received a letter on April 18 1922, in which
Eric reported that he expected to be in Paris from late April
to early May. That was the last communication they had
with their son.

They began to get really anxious about the middle of
June. Revd Tombe wrote to the accommodation address in
Jermyn Street, asking if they had heard from Eric, and
eventually went there himself. They told him the last time
his son had called for his letters had been 20 April, and
they had no forwarding address for him. He then
advertised in two London daily newspapers for information about Eric, but received no replies.

It was about this time that Mrs Tombe began to have
dreams concerning her son.

'Gordon,' said Mrs Tombe one morning over breakfast,
'I had that dream again last night. I saw Eric as plain as I

see you. He was standing by the bed. And I'm sure he was trying to tell me something.'

'What was he trying to tell you, my dear?'

'I don't know. But I had this strong feeling that he was going to say something. And then he just faded away.' Her voice trailed off and her head dropped and she dabbed at her eyes with a lace handkerchief.

After breakfast Revd Tombe went into his study and wrote a letter to Scotland Yard, telling them about his wife's dreams and the fact that they had had no contact with Eric for several months. They heard nothing for several weeks, then a member of the local constabulary came to interview them. He was not very encouraging, however, pointing out that for a young man of twenty-eight not to communicate with his parents for some months was not all that unusual, especially if he had gone abroad.

Mrs Tombe's dreams continued and Revd Tombe decided to go up to London and question people in and around the Haymarket, where his son had last been seen.

One day he passed a barber's shop and on an impulse went in. 'I wonder if you know my son, Eric Tombe?'

'Oh yes sir, I know Mr Tombe very well. He always comes in regular. Lieutenant Tombe we always call him – I think he used to be a lieutenant? He always looks so dashing.'

'Have you seen him lately?'

The barber shook his head. 'Haven't seen him since – when would it be? – March at least, sir.'

'And you don't know where he's gone? You see, his mother and I are getting anxious about him. It's nearly a year since we've heard anything from him.'

'Afraid not, sir. He didn't say anything to me about going away at all.'

'And you don't know of any friends of his I might contact?'

'Sorry, sir.'

Revd Tombe had just opened the door when the barber's voice called him back. 'Just a minute, sir, I've remembered something.'

The parson turned back into the shop.

'There was a chap who sometimes came in with the Lieutenant. Now what was his name? Shorter than him, but a bit flashy-looking, you know, not quite out of the top drawer. Dyer, sir. That was his name, Dyer. I remember now. Said he was the Lieutenant's partner or something.'

'Eric did say something about once having a business partner, but he never said who it was.'

'They had a stud farm, didn't they? I'm sure they did. I remember the Lieutenant talking about it. Yes, it's all coming back now. Somewhere beyond Croydon it was. The Welcomes. Yes, that was it. And I'll tell you something else, sir.' He suddenly became serious. 'There was a fire there.'

It was the first time the Revd Tombe had heard about the fire or the relationship between his son and Dyer. He went back home with his mind in a whirl, but before he had a chance to relate all his news to his wife she stopped him.

'Gordon, before you tell me what you've found out, let me tell you about the dream I had last night. You rushed off in such a hurry this morning that I didn't have a chance to speak to you.'

'I'm sorry, my dear. That was thoughtless of me.' He sat down beside her and took her hand in his. 'You must tell me your dream first.' Although he was convinced that it was the same one he'd heard many times before.

'I dreamed that I saw Eric again. But this time he didn't say anything. His eyes were closed and ... and ... Oh Gordon, I think he was dead!'

Revd Tombe pressed his wife's hand gently while he waited for her to compose herself.

'And ... and I think he was at the bottom of a well!'

The parson thought over all that he had heard that day. 'Tomorrow,' he said, 'I'm going to Scotland Yard.'

Superintendent Francis Carlin took charge of the case

and discovered that Eric Tombe had an account with Lloyds Bank in Bond Street. In the early part of April 1922 it stood at £2,570 and about that time £1,350 was transferred by him to the Paris branch. On 25 April the bank received a letter, purporting to be signed by Eric Tombe and requesting the bank to allow his business partner Ernest Dyer to draw on the account.

This the bank authorized, and Dyer duly began drawing money out. Then, on 7 August, the Bond Street branch received a letter from their Paris branch. It related a visit paid them by Dyer who had produced a power of attorney, apparently signed by Tombe, allowing him to draw on the rest of the account in London. The Bond Street branch transferred funds and Dyer promptly removed money until that too was exhausted. Later, in England, he continued to draw on the account, using cheques with the signature of Eric Tombe, and the cheques had to be returned since there were no funds to meet them.

On a bright day in September 1923 Superintendent Carlin and Detective Inspector Hedges of Z Division paid a visit to The Welcomes stud farm. The path leading to the five-barred gate was now overgrown with weeds and the whole place had an abandoned air. It was obvious that nobody lived there now, nor had done so for many months.

The charred remains of the farmhouse had never been repaired and now stood forlorn and neglected. There was also a cottage on the property, but this too had an unlived-in air and gave no clues to the previous occupants.

'Look for wells,' said Carlin and Hedges glanced at him curiously, for the superintendent had given no clues as to why he was interested in them.

They found five wells or cesspits, all of which had been filled in.

'We'll start tomorrow,' said the superintendent. 'I want these wells emptied.'

The next day several other police officers joined Carlin and Hedges and made a start clearing the tons of rubble, bricks, concrete and general rubbish which filled the shafts. They emptied them one at a time. It was backbreaking work and required a derrick to be set up over each shaft with a pulley and rope attached to it, the rope having a bucket on the end, to lift the debris from the bottom.

It took them two days to empty three pits but towards the end of the second day, with the light going out of the sky, they came across a layer of mud and water at the bottom of the third shaft.

'Careful now,' said Carlin. 'This is the first time we've come across this much earth in the bottom of a well. I want it removed slowly.'

The bucket was sent down, each time coming up filled with water and mud.

'Can you smell anything?' asked Carlin.

Hedges shook his head. 'Just the usual stench of rotting vegetation.'

'We'll go down a bit further.'

The work continued.

Then Carlin stopped the men working and swung a lantern out over the well-top so that it shone down into the bottom of the now dark pit.

'Take a look down there,' he said to Hedges.

The detective inspector took the lantern and swung it out. 'My God!' he said. For there, far below, sticking up from the mud at the bottom was a human foot.

The body was carefully removed and a post-mortem conducted by Dr Stanley Brooke, the divisional surgeon. He reported that the body was in an advanced stage of decomposition and had been in the well for longer than six to eight months. The skull was completely shattered, but by carefully putting together the pieces he was able to say that death had been caused by a shotgun wound in the back of the head.

Revd Tombe identified the body as that of his son by the presence of a gold wristwatch, on the back of which was inscribed the words 'E. Gordon Tombe', and by a gold safety-pin and a silk scarf.

Further investigation by the police turned up Mrs Dyer. She remembered a night in June 1922 when she had been living in the cottage at The Welcomes. She hadn't seen her husband for some days and was under the impression that he was abroad. She heard a sound, coming from outside, like stones being thrown down a drainpipe.

Going out into the darkness she saw a shadowy figure standing near the cowshed and close to the well where the body was later found. She recognized her husband.

'What are you doing here at this time of night, Ernest?'

Dyer jumped noticeably. 'You know very well that with my state of credit I daren't be seen around here in the daylight.'

She persuaded him to come into the cottage, but he wouldn't stay and refused to tell her what he had been doing.

Sometime later Superintendent Carlin and Detective Inspector Hedges were discussing the case. 'All you have to do now,' said the inspector, 'is to find Dyer.'

The superintendent shook his head. 'Haven't you heard? Last November a man called Fitzsimmons was detained in a Scarborough hotel. When the police went up to his room they found a quantity of blank cheques on which the name Eric Tombe had been pencilled. Obviously for inking-in later on. And also two service medals on the backs of which were stamped the words: "Lieutenant E. Dyer".

'But that's not the end of the story. As they were going upstairs to his room with this man Fitzsimmons in the lead, closely followed by an Inspector Abbot, the inspector suddenly noticed the man's left arm move. He caught up with him and they began struggling on the stairs. Abbot yelled for help and a PC, who'd been with him, came up behind and rendered assistance. They all collapsed in a heap on the landing with this man Fitzsimmons underneath.

'Then a shot rang out and the man went limp. When they

turned him over they discovered he had a revolver in his left hand which had been discharged. By the time the doctor and the ambulance arrived the man was dead. Now it's my opinion that when he saw the police, Fitzsimmons, or Dyer, thought they'd come to pick him up for the Tombe murder, which they hadn't, by the way. But whether he shot himself deliberately or by accident we shall never know.'

9   Henriette Caillaux:
Lies, Damn Lies and Politics

'I want to buy a revolver,' said the lady.

The shopkeeper, Monsieur Gastinne-Renette, bowed low. He knew her very well. Who in Paris did not? She was Madame Henriette Caillaux, the wife of the minister of finance and a celebrated society hostess. A small blonde woman in her forties, she was dressed in the height of fashion; and her round face still showed much of the beauty for which she was famed in her youth.

'Of course, madame, a revolver,' murmured the gunsmith. He snapped his fingers and one of his assistants came running up.

'During the coming election I shall be motoring by myself,' continued Mme Caillaux, 'between Paris and my husband's constituency of Mamers, and I feel I need a gun for my protection.'

'Very wise, madame,' agreed the proprietor. But privately he thought the precaution a trifle excessive. This, after all, was March 1914 and footpads had not been seen on the roads outside Paris for many years. On the other hand her husband, Joseph Caillaux, had been the subject of vindictive attacks in the press, notably *Le Figaro*. A leader of the Left, he was committed to the introduction of income tax, a move bitterly resented by the Right. He was also accused of having too many sympathies with

Germany, of which most French nationalists were deeply suspicious. Consequently he was very unpopular in the country. Perhaps Mme Caillaux, being the wife of a public figure undergoing such vilification, feared that her own life was in danger.

'Now here is a very nice little weapon.' M. Gastinne-Renette took a revolver from his assistant and turned it over in his hands, demonstrating the trigger action.

'May I try it?' she asked.

'Of course, madame.' He passed the gun to her.

But the weapon looked very large in her small hand as she struggled with it. 'Oh, that will not do, M. Gastinne-Renette. I have hurt my finger trying to pull the trigger!'

'Mon Dieu, how terrible!' He turned to his assistant, his face angry. 'How could you have given us this most unsuitable weapon? Quick, immediately, fetch madame the Browning! Now this, madame,' he said as the young man scurried away to do his master's bidding, 'has a much easier pull.'

When Mme Caillaux eventually took the new gun she looked at it with approval and clicked the trigger several times. 'This is much better. Why didn't you give me this one before? No matter, I want to try this out properly.'

'With the greatest of pleasure, madame. If madame will follow me I will conduct her downstairs to our shooting gallery, where she can try the weapon to her heart's content.'

Mme Caillaux showed that she was no mean markswoman. She put six bullets in a small group in the metal target at the other end of the range. Then she handed the revolver to the assistant standing by her side. 'Show me how to reload, please. Then I will purchase it.'

A short time later she walked out of the shop with the gun and a box of cartridges concealed in her muff, entered the large grey car which had been waiting for her at the kerb and ordered the chauffeur to drive home. There she wrote a brief note to her husband and gave it to her daughter's English governess, with instructions to pass it over to him if she had not returned by seven o'clock. Then she summoned the car again. This time she instructed her driver to take her to the offices of *Le Figaro*.

It was just after five o'clock in the afternoon when the car pulled up outside 26 Rue Drouot. Mme Caillaux alighted and swept into the reception area of the great national newspaper.

'Please take me to your editor, M. Gaston Calmette.'

The lady refused to give her name, but the receptionist still made enquiries for her. But he had to report that M. Calmette was not in the building.

'If madame would care to wait?'

Mme Caillaux was conducted to the waiting-room and sat beneath a portrait of the King of Greece. She made a striking picture herself, with a string of matched pearls round her neck, ostrich plumes in her hat and on her lap the large fur muff.

She waited an hour before she heard that Calmette had come in. During this time, it was later claimed, she heard some employees of the newspaper discussing a juicy story about her husband, which they were to publish tomorrow.

Enquiring of a uniformed official if he would tell Calmette that a lady wished to speak with him, she was told, 'He will receive you only if you let him know your name.'

Mme Caillaux reluctantly withdrew a card from her purse and, placing it in an envelope, handed it to the official.

Gaston Calmette had only just come into his office with a friend, Paul Bourget, and was about to leave again to go to dinner when the envelope was handed to him. He looked at the card and passed it to his friend.

'You're not going to receive her, are you?' said Bourget. 'Since you're running this campaign against her husband, won't you be compromising yourself if you see her?'

Calmette shrugged his shoulders. 'I can't refuse to see a lady,' he remarked rather sententiously and, turning to the uniformed official, said: 'Show her in.'

Bourget made a gesture of impatience and left by another door, just as Mme Caillaux entered the room.

The uniformed official closed the door behind her, but still had his hand on the handle when something happened which he would remember for the rest of his life.

Shots crashed out from inside the office.

After standing in shocked immobility for a moment he turned and rushed back into the room. M. Calmette was lying behind his desk. Mme Caillaux appeared to be standing over him with a revolver in her hand. As the official approached two more shots were fired. He came up behind and, bravely gripping her arm, managed to wrest the gun from her.

She turned to him, quite calmly. 'I am Mme Caillaux,' she said haughtily. Then added rather enigmatically: 'There is no justice. So I gave it.'

It was discovered afterwards that she had fired six shots – the whole magazine. Two had gone harmlessly into a bookcase, but the other four had hit Calmette. One bullet had passed into his abdomen and ruptured an artery. He was mortally wounded. The staff who came rushing into the room lifted him into a chair and loosened his clothing, but there was little they could do for him.

The police eventually arrived together with an ambulance, and Calmette was driven to a hospital where he died later that night. Mme Caillaux was taken to the police station in the Rue du Faubourg in her own car.

Joseph Caillaux was at the Finance Ministry when the telephone rang and he learned the news of the tragedy. He immediately ordered a taxi and went to the police station where his wife was being held. By this time, news of the shooting had spread all over Paris and an unruly mob surrounded the police station.

As Caillaux stepped from his taxi he was jostled by the unfriendly crowd. He pushed through them and up to the entrance of the station.

Caillaux was allowed a few minutes with his wife.

'What have you done, my dear?' he said clasping her cold hands in his.

She threw herself into his arms and pressed her tear-stained face against his coat. Eventually she recovered herself. 'I hope he's not dead,' she said. 'I didn't mean to kill him.'

Caillaux gently sat her down on the narrow iron bedstead in the cell and positioned himself beside her. 'What made you do such a terrible thing?'

Mme Caillaux dabbed at her eyes with a handkerchief. 'Well, you know in the car today, as I was picking you up from the Ministry to go to lunch, and I told you that I'd been to see Judge Monier ... He told me there was no legal means of putting an end to the campaign that *Le Figaro* is running against you?'

'Yes, yes, I remember all that, my dear,' said the minister impatiently. 'What about it?'

'Do you remember that you flew into a rage and declared: "Very well then, I'll go and break his neck" I said: "When?" and you answered: "In my own good time."'

'Yes! Yes!'

'Well, I ...'

'Oh, my poor little thing,' said Caillaux, folding his wife into his arms.

Joseph Caillaux was a small practically bald man who looked like Agatha Christie's Hercule Poirot. Quick-tempered and quixotic, he was voluble and high-spirited. He went straight from seeing Mme Caillaux to telephone the prime minister and resign his cabinet position, in order to devote himself to his wife's defence.

Mme Caillaux was interviewed by an examining magistrate. The procedure in France was that this official interrogated the accused and had wide powers to summon and question any witnesses he chose. He then decided if there was a case to answer and if so the accused was committed to the assizes for trial.

At the trial there was a jury, as in the British system, and a number of judges of whom the chief, or president of the court, conducted the cross-examination of the prisoner and witnesses. There were also counsels for both prosecution and defence and lawyers who represented the victim's relatives and whose job it was to secure damages for them, or to clear the victim's name if any slurs had been cast upon it.

The trial of Mme Caillaux began, before the Assize Court of the Seine, on Monday, 20 July 1914. M. Jean-Marie Albanel was the president of the court and M. Herbaux the prosecuting counsel. Maître Labori, the famous lawyer who had defended Dreyfus and Zola, appeared for the defence. Maître Chenu represented the relatives of M. Calmette.

It was a feature of French courts that the rules of evidence were very wide and encompassed all manner of depositions. Witnesses were allowed to make statements, present arguments and hearsay evidence, and even dispute evidence given by other witnesses.

When Mme Caillaux entered the dock all eyes were drawn to her. She was dressed in a dark costume relieved by a mauve corsage and from her black hat twin plumes rose like black wings. Her round face was pale under her blonde hair and she wore long black kid gloves.

The president of the court asked her to repeat the personal particulars which she had given at the preliminary enquiry.

She began by describing her early life, reporting that she had been educated at home and had not left until she had married. Her first husband, a M. Clairtie, was a literary critic. From the very beginning there had been difficulties in the marriage. In 1908 she was granted a divorce, together with the custody of her children. One later died. She then went on to relate how, in 1911, she had married M. Joseph Caillaux.

Then, twisting a minute black-bordered handkerchief in her small hands, she went on to speak of the campaign against her husband in the press, which had poisoned her life.

'Everywhere we were slandered,' she said, dabbing her eyes with the little handkerchief. 'In the drawing-rooms of the city, in the Chamber, in the shops, everywhere. At my dressmaker's I was pointed out to customers as the wife of that beast Caillaux!' She pressed her hands to her eyes in a gesture of agony.

'This *Figaro* campaign was implacable,' she told the court, raising and lowering her arms in an almost hysterical gesture. 'Every day! Every day! Since the beginning of the year there have been 138 articles in *Le Figaro* attacking my husband. I could hardly sleep. I was tortured by fear – the fear that my husband would be murdered. I heard it was common everywhere to hear regrets that no one had the pluck to rid the country of this disgrace to France!'

It was here that the president of the court interrupted. 'The campaign seems to have had a political character. You say that it was personal. Will you explain to the jury why you think so?'

'Surely, Monsieur Le President, no one who has read all the articles in the *Figaro* could possibly maintain they were political! Calmette accused my husband of using dishonourable means to serve his political ambitions. He accused him of selling the French Congo to the Germans for a large sum of money and said that a coronet worth F750,000 (about £30,000) had been given to me by the German Emperor. That is a lie!

'But worst of all,' – and here her voice dropped almost to a whisper – 'Calmette plumbed the depths of depravity by publishing the first of the three letters which appeared in *Le Figaro*.'

'Will you please tell the jury where the letters came from and the circumstances in which they were written?' asked M. Albanel.

The small figure in the dock hesitated, but then she began. 'My husband was already an influential figure in the House of Deputies when, in 1900, he formed an association with a young married woman, Berthe Dupré. He didn't really want to marry, but nevertheless wrote her some rather indiscreet letters. It was one of those that Calmette got hold of and actually published in his newspaper: the so-called *"Ton Jo"* ["Your Jo"] letter. I should emphasize that the letter was written thirteen years ago and was only used by Calmette to try and embarrass my husband.'

Mme Caillaux, for a moment, seemed overcome and the president gently urged her. 'Please go on with your story, madame.'

'I think it was in 1904 that Berthe Dupré asked her husband for a divorce – against the advice, I may add, of M. Caillaux. Having got what she wanted she then persuaded M. Caillaux to marry her. But he soon realized that it was a mistake. He found her a bad housekeeper. She was extravagant and, worse than that, turned out to be temperamental and difficult to live with. However, he met me at a friend's house when my marriage was in great difficulties and we … became friends.'

There was ribald laughter in the court at this, but ignoring it Mme Caillaux carried on. 'Soon Berthe Caillaux learned of our friendship and there were furious rows between them. Then Joseph wrote me a long letter saying that we must keep our relationship a secret because elections were due soon and his enemies would try to use our friendship to discredit him. But he realized that if the letter fell into the wrong hands it also could be used against him and so he asked me to return it. I did so and he put this letter, together with some I had written to him, in a locked drawer in his desk.

'But during the night his wife forced open the drawer and found the letters. She immediately began to use them against him, threatening to make them public unless he gave me up entirely. He was forced to agree to her terms. But he made a bargain with her. He would stop seeing me if she destroyed the letters. She agreed to this and they were burned in the presence of witnesses. They then went off on holiday together.

'But the perfidy of the woman was unbounded. Joseph soon discovered that she had kept photographic copies of the letters. He was furiously angry and left her immediately, returning home alone. Finally, he obtained a divorce after first paying her a large sum of money. Again all letters were burned and this time she signed a declaration before an attorney that she had kept no copies.

'Joseph and I were married in October 1911. But we hadn't realized how vindictive that woman could be. Her treachery was immeasurable! We heard just after we were married that the woman had offered copies of the letters to two newspapers, but they were both too honourable and refused to publish them. Then we learned that Calmette was negotiating for them. But we did not think he would publish them either until the *"Ton Jo"* letter appeared. We realized then that there were no depths to which he would not sink!

'On 16 March, after the publication of the *"Ton Jo"* letter, he performed his most despicable action ever. He hinted in the newspaper that he intended to publish our most intimate letters.'

Judge Albanel then took •Mme Caillaux through the incidents of that fatal day: the morning reading in *Le Figaro* of the forthcoming publication of the intimate letters; the visit of Mme Caillaux to Judge Monier; her meeting with her husband at lunchtime; followed by the buying of the gun and the return home to write the note for her husband.

When they reached this point the judge read out the note to a hushed courtroom.

My beloved husband,

When I told you this morning of my interview with
Judge Monier … you told me that one of these days
you would break the vile Calmette's neck. I know
your decision to be irrevocable. From that instant my
mind was made up. I will see that justice is done.
France and the Republic have need of you. I will carry
out the task! If you should receive this letter it will
mean that I have obtained or tried to obtain justice.
Forgive me, but my patience is at an end. I love you
and I embrace you with all my heart.

Your Henriette.

'Now Mme Caillaux,' said the president of the court, 'the
prosecution claim that this letter, together with the fact
that you deliberately purchased a revolver on the day of
the incident, indicated that the shooting was a premeditated act on your part. Can you give the jury as complete
an explanation as you can of this note?'

Mme Caillaux drew herself up. 'When I wrote the note I
still did not know what I ought to do … When I said in the
note "I will see that justice is done", I did not mean that I
intended to kill him, only to teach him a lesson, cause a
scandal. I have passed my whole life without having the
desire to kill. How could anyone possibly imagine that I
wished to cause his death?'

The next day a witness, M. Latzarus, a journalist
working on *Le Figaro*, introduced a political angle to the
trial.

'In late January,' he said, 'I was in Calmette's office
discussing with him the campaign he was conducting
against Caillaux. Calmette took from his pocket two
handwritten documents and gave them to me to read.
Genlemen, every Frenchman who read them could not fail
to realize the infamy and the treason of the man
implicated in them, Caillaux. But Calmette would not

publish them because to do so would be a danger to the country. This is the man whose character has been so blackened by Mme Caillaux!'

Then Maître Chenu, representing Calmette's relatives, seemed determined to pursue the political line, for he read out in court the *'Ton Jo'* letter.

The important parts of the letter were as follows:

> I had to take my part in two terribly tiring sessions of the Chamber yesterday … However, I secured a magnificent success. I crushed the income tax while appearing to defend it, I received an ovation from the Centre and from the Right, and I managed not to make the Left too discontented. I succeeded in giving the wheel a turn towards the right which was quite indispensable …
>
> Your Jo.

Although it had been written thirteen years before, the letter illustrated Caillaux's indiscretions. It was written, using the affectionate 'tu' form and signed 'ton Jo', to Berthe Dupré who was the wife of another man. And even allowing for the fact that perhaps Caillaux didn't feel the time was then right for introducing income tax, the letter shows a high degree of political duplicity, since he was minister of finance when he wrote it and was supposed to be trying to have income tax introduced.

But the introduction of the *'Ton Jo'* letter and the accusations made against him by Latzarus played into Caillaux's hands. He was an experienced politician, used to arguing political points in public and he seized the opportunity eagerly.

He approached the bar to give his evidence, a small elegant figure with a shining bald head. Marching up to the dock, he kissed his wife's hand in dramatic fashion before taking his place at the bar. When he began to speak he proved to have a high-pitched voice – as one British newspaper described it, like the voice of Mr Winston Churchill without the lisp.

He began by going over his early life and the marriage to Berthe Dupré. Then he described his marriage to Henriette, with warmth. Turning to politics he explained that ever since he first became a Deputy, when he defeated a royalist candidate, he had been the victim of nationalist attacks, but had always ignored them. His wife, however, was most worried by them, especially by the recent attacks in *Le Figaro*. And he blamed himself that he did not notice the campaign was preying on her mind so much.

Caillaux then turned to Calmette's attacks in detail. Their motive he said was undoubtedly to stop the introduction of income tax, to which he (Caillaux) was committed. He then went through each of the charges in detail, arguing that none of them was true.

When he had dealt with the newspaper accusations he began an attack on *Le Figaro* and Calmette himself. He said that when Calmette wanted to become the editor he was backed by a group of financiers who obtained a controlling interest in the company owning the newspaper. And the group was headed by a representative of a German bank! He also accused *Le Figaro* of taking money to reprint articles written by the Austro-Hungarian government, which was a known supporter of Germany.

In vain did M. Prestat, director of *Le Figaro*, deny the charges. The damage had already been done. No longer had the trial any resemblance to the simple prosecution of a woman accused of murdering a newspaper editor. It had now become a political battle between the wily minister Caillaux and the newspaper.

'I should like to ask permission to read Calmette's will,' said Caillaux.

A look of surprise appeared on the president's face. 'However did you obtain that?' he asked.

A slight smile curled Caillaux's lips. 'In the same way, Monsieur Le President, that Calmette obtained the *"Ton Jo"* letter.'

Maître Chenu leaped to his feet. 'I really don't feel that any useful purpose would be served by reading the will.'

'I insist that it is absolutely indispensable to the case,' snapped Caillaux.

Having received permission to quote the will, he went on to inform the court that Calmette had left a fortune of 13 million francs, just over half a million pounds in British money.

'In middle-class families,' declared Caillaux, 'from which Calmette and I come, 150 years would be necessary in the ordinary course of events to accumulate a fortune of this size.'

He also read out a list of investments. 'Mark these carefully,' he advised the jury, 'for these all represent investments on which the honourable Calmette has not paid any tax!'

And so the tables had been turned. The editor who had attacked the honour and integrity of the minister in his newspaper had his own character impugned by Caillaux in court. But he was no longer alive and able to answer the charges.

The issue of the trial was, however, finally resolved, when Caillaux produced some documents which he handed to Judge Albanel.

'Where did you get these?'

'They were given to me, Monsieur Le President, by Count Karolyi, who is the leader of the Independence Party in Hungary, that is the opposition party in that country. And you will note that they are signed by Monsieur Calmette and by a representative of the Hungarian government.

Albanel studied the documents for a while in silence. Then his face began to go red with anger. In a voice shaking with emotion he reported to the court: 'These documents are a contract between Calmette and the Austro-Hungarian government which pledges him to write articles which will serve the interests of that government!'

There was a storm of protest in court. People stood up and shouted: 'Calmette the traitor! Shooting's too good for him!'

In the final speeches of the counsel Maître Labori made an emotional appeal, painting Mme Caillaux as an innocent and helpless figure in the rush and tumult of the political struggle. And at its close the speech was greeted by an outburst of applause.

Then the President asked the jury to consider two questions. 'Was Mme Caillaux guilty of murder, in other words did she intend to kill?' 'And was the murder premeditated?'

It took the jury an hour to find her not guilty on both charges.

The verdict was received with applause and cheering inside the courtroom and as Caillaux went to congratulate his wife he passed through crowds of back-slapping friends.

But outside, in the corridors, an angry crowd of royalists chanted: 'Down with Caillaux!' And, in the streets, when the verdict became known, it was greeted with catcalls and booing. A violent demonstration against the jury began, which had to be broken up by the police.

Next day the sensational verdict was overtaken by the news that Austria had invaded Serbia, signalling the imminent outbreak of the First World War. Public interest soon waned in the Caillaux affair, but many politicians, including Poincaré, the president of the republic, and Clemenceau, remained bitter in their feelings towards Caillaux.

In 1917 Clemenceau became prime minister. Caillaux was arrested and accused of working for the enemy. The charges were ludicrous and soon disposed of, but a series of accusations were levelled at him while he was incarcerated in prison. Eventually, nearly three years after he was first arrested, he was convicted on an obscure charge, first made in the Napoleonic Wars, of having corresponded with the enemy, without criminal intent, but nevertheless detrimental to the situation of France. He was sentenced to three years in prison, which he had already served, and to being deprived of civil rights for ten years.

It was thus a kind of poetic justice that the man who had used his undoubted skill as a politician to get his wife off a murder charge, should find himself convicted on charges trumped up by his political enemies.

10   Jeanne Weber: In the Grip of Evil

In the year 1905, spring came early to Paris, and 5 April was a warm day with a light breeze playing about the narrow streets. It was the best time of year for the people who lived in that hilly part of Montmartre known as the Goutte d'Or: a squalid region of tenements, alleys and sooty factories, where the heat of the summer sun would soon make life unbearable for the inhabitants.

In the late afternoon someone rang the bell outside the gates of the nearby Bretonneau Hospital. The doorkeeper looked out and saw a woman with a shawl round her head and a bundle in her arms.

'Please, can you help me? My baby's dying!'

The doorkeeper drew aside the covering of the bundle and saw that the child's face was almost black and that he was gasping for breath. 'Take him up to the children's ward.'

There, the nurses took charge of the baby and quickly informed the duty doctor, whose name was Saillant. He examined the child and came to the conclusion that he was suffering from acute asphyxia. The child was placed in a cot in the ward and the mother allowed to stay nearby.

Later in the day he examined the child again and saw that he was now recovering. His breathing was easier and the dark purple of his face was becoming less pronounced. The doctor now noticed a longitudinal reddish mark on the child's neck, accentuated on the sides but less so in front, and what looked like a bruise on the back of the neck. Having concluded that someone might have tried to choke the child, he called the mother into his office.

Looking at the documents the nurses had filled in for him, he said: 'You are Mme Charles Weber, is that correct?'

The dull-looking woman sitting opposite nodded her head.

'Tell me what happened to your baby.'

'Well ...' The young woman hesitated.

'Take your time,' said the doctor kindly. 'Tell me the whole story, from the beginning. What did you do today?'

The young woman eventually said. 'My husband and I live at Charenton, just outside Paris, with my baby Maurice.'

The doctor nodded. 'Go on.'

'Today I took Maurice to see my sister-in-law, Jeanne. She lives in the Goutte d'Or.' Her eyes suddenly over-flowed with tears, but she brushed them away irritably. 'Since she lost her own son she's always asking me to call by and show her my baby – he's ten months now, by the way. Another sister-in-law, Mme Pierre Weber, came with me.'

'How many sisters-in-law have you got?'

The young mother cleared her throat. 'There's four Weber brothers. Jean, whose wife is Jeanne – they live in the Passage of the Goutte d'Or. Then there's Pierre, whose wife came with me today, and Léon and finally my husband Charles.'

'Go on with your story,' said the doctor having written down all this information.

'Jeanne gave us lunch. Then, after the meal, Jeanne, who suffers with her legs, said she wanted some shopping done, so I went to buy her some needles and my other sister-in-law to get her some wine.'

'She likes a drink then, your sister-in-law?'

The doctor could see by the way that the young woman coloured that he had hit the nail on the head. Like many women living in that squalid and depressing area Jeanne Weber probably drank heavily.

'What happened then? You left the baby with Mme Jean?'

Tears again appeared in the young woman's eyes and coursed unheeded down her cheeks. 'Mme Pierre returned after only a few minutes and found ... and found ...'

What she found, the doctor discovered by patient questioning, was the baby, black in the face, foaming at the mouth and obviously choking. Jeanne Weber was sitting beside the child with her hands concealed under the baby's vest. When Mme Charles herself returned a few minutes later she took her child to the hospital.

Dr Saillant sensed that there was something the young mother was not telling him. He did not press her, but allowed several hours to elapse, then examined the baby again. It was making good progress and would be able, he judged, to be discharged in the morning. Mme Charles was now much calmer and he talked to her again. This time he heard the whole story.

It seemed to have begun about a month ago, on Thursday 2 March. That morning, Mme Pierre Weber was going to the public wash-house. Normally she would have asked neighbours to look after her two children, Georgette, who was eighteen months and Suzanne, two years old, but Jeanne had called and immediately offered to look after them. Leaving instructions for the treatment of Georgette, who was suffering from a cough, and Suzanne, who was recovering from the effects of pneumonia, the young mother left for the laundry.

She had only been gone about an hour when a neighbour rushed into the wash-house. 'Mme Pierre! You must come! Georgette is very ill! I heard cries and looked into your home to see the little girl sitting on your sister-in-law's lap choking.'

The young mother rushed home to find her little Georgette lying on the bed with her tongue protruding, her eyes standing out and gasping for breath. Jeanne was stooping over the child with her hands under its clothes trying, as she said, to revive the heart.

Mme Pierre snatched up her child and took it to the window where the fresh air soon revived it. She returned the child to Jeanne with the admonition to take good care of her and went back to the laundry.

An hour later she was recalled again, but this time she was too late. The child was dead.

It was the neighbour, Mademoiselle Pouche, who first noticed dark marks on the child's neck, when she was laying out the body, and she pointed them out to the father, Pierre Weber. He promised to tell the doctor, but the child was buried without further investigation.

Nine days later the process was repeated with the other child. Young Suzanne was left with her Aunt Jeanne and was discovered, this time when her father returned to the house, with a purple face and all the signs of choking. Thinking it was the effects of some cough syrup she'd had that morning, he held the child at the window and she seemed to recover. He returned her to Jeanne Weber's care and went back to work. The result was the death of their second child.

Once again it was the sharp-eyed neighbour who discovered suspicious signs. While helping to undress the body she found that a scarf had been tied round the child's neck and underneath was a long dark mark about the width of a finger.

This time the family were more cautious and the police were called, but the police surgeon ignored the marks and listed the cause of death as 'convulsions'.

Two weeks later, on 25 March, Jeanne went to see her sister-in-law, Mme Léon Weber. She complained of feeling unwell and asked Mme Léon to do some shopping for her. Jeanne was left in charge of the seven-month-old Germaine. The child's grandmother in the flat upstairs soon heard cries and rushed down to discover little Germaine struggling for breath. She took the baby upstairs with her and the child recovered.

After staying for the midday meal with Mme Léon, Jeanne again complained that her legs were troubling her and asked her sister-in-law to go out and buy her some cheese which she needed to take back with her. Again the trusting woman left her baby in Jeanne Weber's care. When she returned little Germaine was again purple-faced and gasping for breath.

Jeanne had her hand pressed upon the child's chest.

A doctor was summoned, but he could find no sign of convulsions. He was puzzled by the appearance of blood under the skin just above the ear, but could suggest no reason for it. He prescribed some medicine and said he would call again the next day. When he did so he found the child much improved.

Jeanne Weber soon arrived, solicitous for the child's health and anxious to help. Incredibly, Mme Léon was again persuaded by Jeanne Weber to leave the baby Germaine in her care while she ran another errand for her sister-in-law. And when Mme Léon returned her child was dead.

It may seem unbelievable that the Weber family continued to leave their children with Jeanne after so many of them had died while in her care. But in the early 1900s infant mortality in that quarter of Paris was very high. And the death of children by choking was not uncommon. But, according to Mme Charles Weber, by that time even the Weber family were entertaining some suspicions towards Jeanne. Then an event occurred which changed the situation dramatically.

Within a few hours of little Germaine Weber's burial Jeanne Weber's own seven-year-old son, Marcel, died in a similar way to all the other Weber children. The doctor diagnosed diphtheria.

In the manner of families everywhere, dark doubts were put aside and all members extended their sympathy to the sorrowing Jeanne. And that no doubt would have remained the situation had it not been for what befell young Maurice, the child of Mme Charles, when he was left with Jeanne Weber. As she ended her story it was plain that Mme Charles was torn between loyalty to her sister-in-law and suspicions as to what had happened to her baby.

On the morning of the next day Dr Saillant noted that the facial colour of the child was back to normal, but there were now distinct blue marks on young Maurice's throat. He called in his superior, Dr Sevestre, and both men examined the child. Neither was an expert in forensic medicine but both were convinced that the marks were the signs of attempted strangulation.

They immediately got in touch with the police. Jeanne Weber was arrested and taken to prison and two police inspectors began an investigation. They discovered that she had been born Jeanne Moulinet on 6 October 1874, in the little Breton fishing village of Keritry. When she was fourteen she had made her way to Paris and become a domestic servant. She married Jean Weber in 1893, when she was nineteen, and they lived at 1, Passage of the Goutte d'Or. In 1902 her two daughters died, but there was no evidence that the deaths were in any way unnatural. There were some suspicions among neighbours, however, that the deaths of two other children, Lucie Alexandre and Marcel Poyatos, who died while in her care, were not natural deaths, although nothing could be proved at this late stage.

After interviewing many people the inspectors were able to confirm Mme Charles's story and when they reported their findings to Examining Magistrate Leydet he was convinced that the Weber children had all been strangled, Maurice escaping only by a lucky accident. He ordered the exhumation of the other children's bodies and autopsies to be performed on each by Dr Léon Henri Thoinot, who would also examine young Maurice.

Professor Thoinot was one of the leading members of the famous faculty of forensic medicine in Paris and, aged forty-seven, was at the top of his profession.

He examined Maurice Weber on 10 April. By that time the marks on the baby's throat had disappeared and the doctor could find no signs of violence on the child. He concluded that he could make no positive observations. It was always possible, the doctor remarked, that the mother's statements were misleading and the child might have suffered ordinary cramp of the glottis. He noted the reports of the doctors at the Bretonneau Hospital but repeated that he could make only negative observations.

Four days later the bodies of Georgette, Suzanne and Germaine Weber were exhumed. Professor Thoinot performed post-mortem examinations on them. He failed to find any visible injuries to the throat of Georgette. He did discover a small effusion of blood on the left side of Suzanne's neck, but he considered it the result of decay rather than an injury received in life. And on Germaine's body he found no signs of violence at all.

He concluded that, although the autopsies had shown no signs of a natural illness leading to death, it could not be inferred that there wasn't any. There were many cases of natural death, he stated, which left no visible changes in the organs and he sited the common glottal cramp of children and pseudodiphtheria.

His post-mortem on the body of Marcel Weber was equally negative. There were no signs of strangulation or choking, and he was sure that he could exclude the possibility that the boy had been murdered by the hand or by a cord.

In his report he stated: '...the facts furnished by the autopsies cannot prove death as a result of criminal violence'.

But Magistrate Leydet remained stubbornly convinced that Jeanne Weber was responsible for the deaths of four children and, on 29 January 1906, nine months after she had first been arrested, she was sent for trial.

The case had already caused a sensation in France and the rest of Europe and even in the United States of America. One of the most brilliant advocates in France, Maître Henri Robert, perhaps realizing the publicity that would be generated by the trial, volunteered to defend Jeanne Weber – although, by this time, she had already been convicted by the people of Paris and was known as 'L'Ogresse'.

The outcome of the trial did not remain in doubt for very long. The doctors who appeared for the prosecution were not experts in forensic medicine and their testimony was ridiculed by the defence counsel. On the other hand, Dr Thoinot had the weight of prestige on his side and he was ably supported by colleagues from the faculty of forensic medicine. By the afternoon of only the second day the prosecuting counsel himself conceded defeat and recommended a verdict of not guilty.

As is sometimes the case with heavily reported trials, during the proceedings public opinion had swung completely round and the verdict was greeted with shouts of approval and prolonged applause. Jean Weber broke down and clutched the hands of Maître Robert. Through tear-dimmed eyes she looked round the crowded room and caught sight of her husband sitting in the body of the court.

She shouted to him, 'I did not kill them! Say you believe me now!'

His reply could not be heard above the noise, but he climbed over the benches and seized his plump wife in his arms.

But though Jean Weber had made a public demonstration of confidence in his wife, in private his faith in her

soon began to wane. Indeed the whole of the Weber clan
started to turn against her. They kept their children away
from her and so did all their neighbours. This was a bitter
blow. In June, Jeanne Weber and her husband parted.

One cold night in April of the following year in the little
town of Villedieu, 150 miles south of Paris, a little girl
knocked at the door of Dr Papazoglou.

'Please come. My little brother August is very sick.'

Her name was Louise Bavouzet, the daughter of a poor
farm-worker who lived some miles away. The doctor
questioned her and learned that her brother, a boy of nine,
had just been to a neighbour's wedding-party and had
eaten a great deal. He therefore gave her some stomach
medicine for the boy and sent her home.

But the next morning the boy's father himself appeared
at the doctor's house and entreated him to come and see
his son. The doctor did so, but it was only to find the boy
dead in bed.

By the side of the bed, like a greedy spider, sat a plump
young woman with black eyes.

'I'm sorry about your son,' said the doctor.

The woman said nothing, merely looked at the doctor
steadily. But from behind the medical man there came a
cough. Bavouzet, the peasant, had followed him into the
room and stood twisting his cap in his hands. He coughed
again, 'She's … ah … Mlle Moulinet, my … er …
housekeeper.'

Dr Papazoglou merely nodded and bent to examine the
body. He turned to the woman. 'This child has recently
been washed and has a clean nightshirt on.'

'He was sick all down the other one,' replied Mlle
Moulinet sulkily.

The doctor noticed that the nightshirt was fastened
tightly round the throat and he loosened and pulled it
open. There, running almost round the entire neck, was a
reddish mark. The doctor's face wore a puzzled look.

'Will you give us a death certificate?' enquired Mlle Moulinet. 'So we can have the child buried?'

'Perhaps tomorrow,' muttered Dr Papazoglou.

The next day the mark was even clearer and now black in colour. The doctor reported the matter to the police.

Examining Magistrate Belleau had the body removed to the cemetery chapel in Villedieu and asked Dr Charles Audiat, the local police surgeon, to perform an autopsy. During the examination Dr Audiat also noticed the discoloration round the throat, but observing that the mark corresponded so closely with the neck of the nightshirt, he was unsure that it had been caused by anything else. And learning that the child had been ill for some days before he died the doctor considered the death was natural, resulting from convulsions.

The little boy was buried. But at the funeral the dead boy's elder sister Germaine gazed at Mlle Moulinet with hate-filled eyes. She was deeply resentful of this woman who had taken her mother's place and who now shared the family bed with her father.

A few days later, while the older woman was out, she went through the small bag in which Mlle Moulinet kept her meagre belongings. She found some cuttings from the *Petite Parisien* newspaper from two years before. And there, staring up at her from the pictures in the paper, was the face of Mlle Moulinet, the Ogress of the Goutte d'Or.

The child took the cuttings to the police in Villedieu. 'That's the woman who strangled my brother!' she said.

The police soon confirmed that Mlle Moulinet was in fact Mme Jeanne Weber and Examining Magistrate Belleau decided to reopen the case. He called in another doctor, Dr Bruneau, a pathologist, to conduct another autopsy, and the body was exhumed. Dr Bruneau and Dr Audiat did the examination together. This time they found unmistakable evidence of strangulation, an inch-wide furrow round the neck and blood clots in the larynx and the muscles of the neck. They concluded that the child had been strangled, possibly by a handkerchief being twisted round the neck.

At the beginning of May Jeanne Weber was again arrested.

The news soon reached Paris and the newspapers were filled with the new developments in the saga of Jeanne Weber. Maître Henri Robert immediately offered to defend Jeanne Weber again and demanded that the most eminent forensic scientist in the country, Dr Thoinot, be allowed to do an autopsy on the child. The doctor was only too willing to defend his professional reputation and readily agreed to perform the autopsy.

Belleau was reluctantly forced to allow Thoinot to do another examination of the child's body and, at the end of July, some 3½ months after the child's death, Thoinot and his assistant performed their autopsy.

In the report that he subsequently submitted, he had to admit that the process of decay had so changed the tissues in the neck that it was impossible for him to make precise observations. But he then went on to castigate the provincial doctors. So incompetent were they, he insisted, that they had not noticed the evidence for natural death. He claimed that when he had examined the intestines he found clear evidence of typhoid fever.

Audiat and Bruneau, although they argued the point, had to admit that they had not actually examined the intestines. They had merely felt them from the outside. Once again the clever Thoinot had outwitted the opposition.

The examining magistrate appealed to three other eminent pathologists, but they ruled on the case without doing an autopsy themselves. After examining the reports of Dr Thoinot and the two provincial doctors they came down in favour of their famous colleague.

Belleau was forced to admit that there was again a very weak case against Jeanne Weber, and she was accordingly released in December 1907.

So great was the public sympathy for Jeanne Weber that Georges Bonjeau, a well-known philanthropist and president of the Society for the Protection of Children, wishing to make up, as he put it, 'for the wrongs which have been done to this unfortunate woman', gave her a job as an assistant in his children's home in Orgeville. Within a few days, however, she was caught trying to strangle one of the patients. She was quietly sent away. And Bonjeau, afraid perhaps of incurring the wrath of the judicial and medical etablishments, said nothing to the police.

Jeanne Weber then began wandering again. In March 1908 she was arrested as a vagrant in Paris. She immediately identified herself as Jeanne Weber and confessed to having murdered the children in the Goutte d'Or. Since she had already been acquitted of this crime and could not be recharged with it she was questioned about the death of August Bavouzet, with which she had not been charged.

'Oh no,' she replied. 'I didn't kill him, only the Webers.'

The police chief who interviewed her sent her to a mental institution, to be examined by a doctor there, but he pronounced her sane. She was again released.

On 8 May a working man appeared at an inn in Commercy a small town some 160 miles east of Paris. He asked for a room.

'Certainly, sir,' said the innkeeper, and, noting the woman standing behind the workman, added, 'Double?'

'Yes. My name is Emile Bouchery and this is my wife.' He pushed forward the plump dark-haired woman.

The innkeeper shrugged his shoulders and wrote down their names.

'Can we have a meal? I'm a lime-burner and I've just got a job at the quarries, but I've to go back to work soon, and then I won't be in till late.'

Bouchery and the woman had their meal and the man

went off to work. The woman, who seemed very fond of children, began playing with the innkeeper's little son Marcel. When the little boy's bed-time arrived the woman said that she was nervous about sleeping alone and could the child sleep with her? The kindly innkeeper's wife agreed and the woman and the little boy departed, hand in hand, up the stairs.

Later that night another lodger, a Mlle Curlet, who had also gone to bed early, heard the screams of a child coming from the woman's bedroom. The lodger banged on the door, but it was locked and the screaming continued. She rushed downstairs to tell the innkeeper and his wife. They had a duplicate key and soon opened the bedroom door.

A ghastly sight met their eyes.

There, in the bed, lay the little boy. His face was purple and blood was pouring from his mouth where he had nearly bitten through his tongue. Beside him lay the woman, her hands and petticoat covered in blood. Bloodstained handkerchiefs were found stuffed underneath the bed.

A doctor was called, but he was too late to save the child, who died soon after. The police were summoned, and when the woman was searched, a letter dated December 1907 was found on her from Maître Henri Robert addressed to Jeanne Weber, congratulating her on her impending release from prison.

Examining Magistrate Rollin decided to take no chances. He ordered the child's body to be taken to the hospital under guard and photographs to be taken of it immediately. Nobody was going to be able to dispute the facts this time. He asked Professor Parisot of the University of Nancy to come quickly and conduct the autopsy.

He brought with him Professor Michel, the pathologist from the university, and the autopsy was conducted the next day. This time the evidence was there for all to see. A strangulation groove ran round the whole of the neck. On the chin and face were marks clearly made by fingernails. And the imprint of the child's teeth could clearly be seen on the tongue. All the evidence was carefully photographed.

Professor Parisot and Professor Michel issued a joint declaration. Death was caused by strangulation, the means a handkerchief twisted under the chin.

Yet in spite of all this evidence, and the many witnesses who had seen Jeanne Weber virtually strangling the child, she was never brought to trial. Once again the influence of Dr Thoinot played a considerable part in subsequent events. She was examined by two professors, declared insane and on 25 October 1908, confined in an asylum at Maréville.

Two years later she committed suicide.

Bibliography

Archer, Fred, *Killers in the Clear* (W.H. Allen, 1971)

Bechhofer, Roberts, C.E., *Famous American Trials* (Jarrolds, 1947)

Bennett, Benjamin and Rousseau, François, Pierre, *Up For Murder* (Hutchinson, 1934)

Beveridge, Peter, *Inside the C.I.D.* (Evans Brothers, 1957)

Browne, Douglas G. and Tullett, E.V., *Bernard Spilsbury* (Harrap, 1951)

Butler, Ivan, *Trials of Brian Donald Hume* (David & Charles, 1976)

Carlin, Francis, *Reminiscences of an Ex-Detective* (Hutchinson, 1927)

Cassity, John Holland, *The Quality of Murder* (The Julian Press, New York, 1958)

Casswell, J.D., *A Lance for Liberty* (Harrap, 1961)

———, *Only Five Were Hanged* (Corgi, 1964)

Dearden, Harold, *Aspects of Murder* (Staples Press, 1951)

Furneaux, Rupert, *Courtroom U.S.A. 1* (Penguin, 1962)

———, *Famous Criminal Cases 6* (Odhams Press, 1960)

———, *The Medical Murderer* (Elek Books, 1957)

———, *They Died by a Gun* (Herbert Jenkins, 1962)

Graeme, Bruce, *Passion, Murder and Mystery* (Hutchinson, 1927)

Gribble, Leonard, *Murders Most Strange* (John Long, 1959)

———, *Stories of Famous Modern Trials* (Arthur Barker, 1970)

Harrison, Richard, *Criminal Calendar* (Jarrolds, 1951)

Hastings, Macdonald, *The Other Mr Churchill* (Harrap, 1963)

Hatherill, George, *A Detective's Story* (Andre Deutsch, 1971)

Heppenstall, Rayner, *A Little Pattern of French Crime* (Hamish Hamilton, 1969)

House, Jack, *Murder Not Proven?* (Richard Drew, 1984)

Jackson, Robert, *Francis Camps* (Hart-Davis MacGibbon, 1975)

Kershaw, Alister, *Murder in France* (Constable, 1955)

Lane, Brian, *The Murder Club Guide to the Midlands* (Harrap, 1988)

————, *The Murder Club Guide to South-East England* (Harrap, 1988)

Langford, Gerald, *The Murder of Stanford White* (Victor Gollancz, 1963)

Lindsay, Philip, *The Mainspring of Murder* (John Long, 1958)

Murray, Sir James A.H., *A New Dictionary on Historical Principles* (Oxford at the Clarendon Press, 1919)

Orchard-Halliwell, J., *Dictionary of Archaic Provincial Words* (Reeves & Turner, 1889)

Raphael, John N., *The Caillaux Drama* (Max Goschen, 1914)

Roughead, William, *Classic Crimes* (Cassell, 1962)

Sanders, Bruce, *They Couldn't Lose the Body* (Herbert Jenkins, 1966)

Shankland, Peter, *Death of an Editor* (William Kimber, 1981)

Simpson, Keith, *Forty Years of Murder* (Harrap, 1978)

Smith, Sir Sydney, *Mostly Murder* (Harrap, 1959)

Symons, Julian, *A Reasonable Doubt* (The Cresset Press, 1960)

Taylor, Bernard and Knight, Stephen, *Perfect Murder* (Grafton, 1987)

Thaw, Harry K., *The Traitor* (Dorrance, 1926)

Thorwald, Jürgen, *Dead Men Tell Tales* (Thames & Hudson, 1966)

Totterdell, G.H., *Country Copper* (Harrap, 1956)

Tullett, Tom, *Portrait of a Bad Man* (Evans Brothers, 1956)

Walls, H.J., *Expert Witness* (John Long, 1972)

Webb, Duncan, *Crime Is My Business* (Frederick Muller, 1953)

———, *Deadline for Crime* (Frederick Muller, 1955)

Williams, John, *Hume: Portrait of a Double Murderer* (Heinemann, 1960)

Wilson, John Gray, *Not Proven* (Secker & Warburg, 1960)

The files of *Berrow's Worcester Journal, Bloemfontein Friend, Daily Express, Daily Mirror, Hampshire Telegraph* and *Post, Johannesburg Star, Le Figaro, le Matin, L'Illustration, New York Evening Post, New York Herald, New York Times, People, Portsmouth Evening News, Pretoria News, Scarborough Evening News* and *Daily Post, The Scotsman, Southport Guardian, Southport Journal, Sunday Pictorial, Surrey Advertiser* and *County Times, Surrey Mirror* and *County Post, The Times, Worcester Herald.*

Index